LISTENING FOR
SMALL SOUNDS

Penelope Trevor, born in Australia in
1960, known as Pepe, lives with her
two children Tashi and Jaspar. *Listening for Small Sounds* is her first novel,
she has recently completed her first
film script and has written numerous
episodes for children's television.
Trained at the V.C.A., she is also a
talented actress. Penelope works in
her gypsy wagon, surrounded by a
dog, three birds, two fish and the
laughter and squabble of her children.

LISTENING FOR SMALL SOUNDS

PENELOPE TREVOR

ALLEN & UNWIN

Lyrics from *Fly me to the Moon*—Bart Howard (Essex 100%) are reproduced by permission of Essex Music of Australia Pty Ltd. Unauthorised reproduction is illegal. The author and publishers would also like to acknowledge their debt to William Shakespeare's *The Tempest* and Banjo Paterson's 'The Swagman's Rest' and 'The Man from Snowy River'.

Publication of this title was assisted by The Australia Council, the Federal Government's arts funding and advisory body.

Australia Council
for the Arts

First published in 1996 by
Allen & Unwin
9 Atchison Street
St Leonards NSW 2065
Australia
Phone: (61 2) 9901 4088
Fax: (61 2) 9906 2218
E-mail: frontdesk@allen-unwin.com.au
URL: http://www.allen-unwin.com.au

National Library of Australia
Cataloguing-in-Publication entry:

Trevor, Penelope, 1960– .
  Listening for small sounds.

  ISBN 1 86448 145 5.

  I. Title.

A823.3

Set in 10.5/13 pt Palatino by DOCUPRO, Sydney
Printed by Australian Print Group, Maryborough, Victoria

10 9 8 7 6 5 4 3 2

Acknowledgements

To my friend and editor, Kate Cole-Adams, who believed in me before there was anything but me to believe in and gave freely of her time, craft and love.

And to my mother, Marie Trevor, who shared the journey with me and never faltered in her encouragement.

A special thankyou to Peter Hepworth, my friend and mentor.

For my children, Jaspar and Tashi

Carlton 1969

She knows the smell of it. Not just of Lygon Street, that smells of cheese and coffee and chocolate melting in the summer sun, but of the back alleys where she plays. They smell of cat piss and are always damp, and in the dirt between the cobbled stones are pieces of broken things. In the park out the front of her house the smell of grass is like a whisper, pushing itself between the stronger smells of people's lives.

Nine-year-old Joss knows a lot about people from the smells that come from their front doors and windows.

Maria spends her life chasing things out of her house: germs with buckets of bleach and her husband with the broom. But only on Saturdays when his whiskers have grown and he has the sweet smell of wine about him. Maria leaves nothing to chance. She has eyes in the back of her head. She never lets one tomato drop to the ground and rot, forgotten. She puts bags over all the little green tomatoes to make sure they ripen together and then together they go into a pot. For three days at the end of summer Joss smells Maria bottling sunshine.

On the corner is a milk bar. The owner is little. His name is Joe and he is from Malta. He is building a boat in his concrete backyard. When he works on the boat, Joss can smell his dreams in the fumes from the oxy-welder. They are of a big man on a blue sea, looking up at green hills covered in orange trees.

And Joss knows that the tall Indian girl has left the tall white boy two houses up when no more smells come from their house. He comes in and tells her mother about it a couple of weeks later. Her mother is shocked. Joss sits at the top of the stairs and listens. He tells her mother everything in a rumbling whisper. When he goes her mother shakes her head.

'He's such a gentle boy,' she says and walks through to the kitchen, to finish cleaning the fridge with warm water and vanilla, before unpacking the shopping. Joss slides down the stairs on her bottom.

It's a small house they live in, a dolls' house really. The last of three identical tiny terraces that share one roof and one garden. Joss goes through the kitchen past her mother who has her head in the fridge, and out the back door.

The garden is overgrown with eucalyptus and cold with the shadows of late afternoon. Joss gathers twigs and dry leaves and builds a small fire in an old tin box. She gets her paints from the woodshed and colours her legs and arms reddy brown, like an Indian. She feeds the fire.

Joss likes pretending she's an Indian, she doesn't like cowboys. Indians know things. They stand on the edge of mountains and listen to the wind. They are beautiful and they have long hair. Joss has short hair, her father likes it that way. Joss goes inside for an apple to cook on a stick over her fire.

Fleshy promises, that this week will be different, tumble from butcher paper onto the kitchen bench; a leg of lamb for a Sunday roast, a chicken, sausages and a piece of steak for Richard tonight, for Daddy.

Her mother lights the griller. They are having sau-

2

sages. Joss reaches across the bench, her legs dangling. Her father's steak is on an old plate with faded roses, next to the fruit bowl. Joss likes that plate, roses of lost red, staining a bone porcelain sky. Once there were leaves.

'Get off the bench JJ.' Joss grabs an apple and jumps down.

'Do you like roses, Mum?'

'What? . . . Oh yeah, I do.' Her mother pricks the sausages.

'Can we plant one?'

'Maybe. One day. JJ don't eat that now. You'll spoil your dinner. Go and hop in the bath.'

Joss and her father planted spring onions once. They moved before the onions grew.

The pink light of dusk fades slowly to darkness; but the smell of the sun is there, captured in the scratchy towel her mother wraps her in.

The front door slams shut.

Joss looks at her mother. Her mother has stilled her body. She is listening, like an animal, for small sounds. Sounds that slide almost unheard, across the radio's rich promise.

'Fly me to the moon and let me play among the stars.'

Ice tinkles into a glass. Joss hears it too.

The ice cracks. Her father has poured himself a drink. Joss imagines him standing in the lounge room moving the liquid round and round in the glass before he sips.

Her mother stands.

'Put your jammies on honey. Dinner's ready.'

Joss sits at the dining-room table, eating. She watches her mother and father in the lounge room. Her father is in a mood. He paces. Angry words come out of his mouth. When he's like this Joss always notices his mouth, the nicotine stains on his teeth. When he's not, she notices his eyes.

Joss's earliest memory is of her father's eyes. The smell of greasepaint and her father's face reflected in a big grubby mirror surrounded by lights, his eyes bright. He'd been happy. He'd been someone else. Joss's father is an actor.

In the lounge room he pauses. He turns to refill his glass.

Her mother swallows as though she has a bad taste in her mouth Joss knows it is the taste of him.

On the beat he turns.

'Fuck them! I'm a bloody good writer and a damn good actor. What the hell would they know!'

Her mother almost misses her cue.

'Yes, you are.' she says.

A beat, before the steel goes out of his shoulders and he sits down. Leaning back in the big black armchair he sips his drink. Joss hardly dares breathe lest she do the wrong thing. But sometimes nothing can be the wrong thing. Her mother walks across the room and lays her hand gently on her father's shoulder. He takes another sip of his drink and stares into the fire. Joss thinks her mother is very brave.

Her mother says, 'It's not really him when he's like that. It's just something in his brain that snaps.' And she tells Joss the story about the black dog that lived next-door when she was a child. The gentle, loyal dog who was fed a bait and went crazy and bit his owner. And of the sadness in the dog's eyes, when all the fight went out of him, just before he died.

Suddenly her father reaches up and pulls her mother onto his lap.

'What the fuck.' He laughs.

4

Her mother pulls back slightly.

He holds her mother's wrist, he has a smile on his face. 'They've asked me to produce,' he says. Her mother gives a little laugh and looks confused.

'But. But that's wonderful,' she says.

He holds her look. 'Is it?'

'Oh yes,' she says. 'It is. You'll be a wonderful producer.'

Joss pushes back her chair and runs into the lounge room.

'Oh yes Daddy. It's wonderful!'

He strokes her head with his big hand. It rests around her throat, his thumb under her chin.

'My little mouse,' he says. 'What's wonderful?'

'Whatever it is!'

He laughs.

They celebrate with ice-cream. Her father has port on his.

'Bedtime,' says her mother clearing away the bowls.

'Goodnight Daddy.' Joss kisses her father. He tickles her and she squirms like a little worm. Her Daddy's a rough tickler.

'Come on.' Her mother's halfway up the stairs.

Blankets down and teddy in. Soft old sheets lining heavy woollen blankets. Ten pats and a kiss before the light goes out. Her mother turns in the doorway.

'See you later alligator' she says.

'In a while crocodile' whispers Joss. She doesn't want to move. Doesn't want to shake away the feeling of her mother's hand resting on her back.

'Hope you smile half a mile,' says her mother, sending love into the darkness. Joss rubs her feet together like a little cricket.

'I will. Goodnight.'

Her mother goes downstairs, into the kitchen, to cook

her father's dinner. Joss can hear her father in the lounge room fixing himself another drink. He calls up to her.

'Sleep tight and make sure the bugs don't bite.'

Joss's heart jumps. She's up. Covers back. Checking.

'I will . . . Goodnight. Love you Daddy.'

Joss looks under her bed, there are shadows in the darkness.

The Pub

'You cunning old bastard. Look at you. A fucking television producer. You've got a proper job.'

Her father looks across the rim of his beer glass at his drunken mate. Joss looks across the rim of her raspberry lemonade glass at her father.

'Two more thanks Jack,' says her father in his best English voice, the one that sets him apart from the rest. Lots of people, mostly actors, come into the pub. They all come up and talk to her father. Some even slap him on the back.

'Gidday Dick.'

'Richard. How's it going?'

'Well done, mate. Well done.' Her father sips his beer and nods at them, his right eye half-closed against the smoke of his cigarette, his left eye smiling.

When they leave the pub it is dark.

'Bastards,' her father mutters as he takes Joss's hand and crosses the road to their car. Her mother walk-runs in small steps behind them.

'They didn't mean anything Richard. They're pleased for you.'

Her father lets go of Joss's hand and opens the back door of the car. Joss gets in.

'I'd like to know where they were a year ago, when we were living in a fucking tent.' He slams the door to emphasize his words. Her parents get in the front.

'It was two years ago,' says her mother quietly. 'And you wouldn't let me tell anyone where we were.'

Her father crunches the gears and does a screaming U-ie. Joss sits back. She'd always thought they'd been happy living in the tent.

When they get home her mother puts Joss to bed. Blankets up and a quick peck. Her mother has her hands full with her father.

In the morning over toast and Coco Pops her mother tells Joss that this new job is exactly what her father needs. Her mother's eyes are cloudy with hope. Joss scratches her nose and looks at her mother.

'Yes, I know,' says her mother. 'You should never hope too hard for anything because being able to hope is more important than any one thing you hope for. It's like believing in God.' Her mother picks up her cup and walks into the kitchen.

'Did your Grandma really used to say that?' asks Joss.

Her mother pours another cup of tea, 'Yes she did. She was Irish.'

There are nights in those first few weeks when her father comes home so excited, with a bunch of tiny pink roses wrapped in purple tissue for her mother, that Joss almost believes it will be alright. Her mother's eyes begin to clear and there's no fighting in the dark.

On Friday nights, after work, her father invites everyone back to their place, to unwind. Her mother feeds them and her father entertains them. He tells stories and organizes carpet golf championships and a game called Killer on the dartboard. Joss sits at the top of the stairs and watches. Everyone drinks a lot and talks about 'the industry.' If wives come, they help Joss's mother in the kitchen, but actresses don't.

When Joss is tired she goes to bed and when her mother can, she sneaks upstairs, to tuck her in. She lies down beside Joss and strokes her head and together they look at the moon. The party going on below.

In the half-light, Joss can see how tired her mother is. But then her mother has to go. She sits up and 'pulls it all together.' By the time she walks out of Joss's bedroom back to the party she doesn't look tired at all.

But after a few weeks come the nights of silent drinking. There are no more roses and in the small house Joss imagines the black dog prowling. She thinks her mother does too, because her mother keeps suggesting they go out. Dinner in Lygon Street, with friends, anything. Her father's better when there's people around.

Joss never says she's tired, wants to go home. She smiles at jokes she doesn't understand and agrees when drunken actors lean on her and tell her how lucky she is. And when they leave the restaurant, Joss always takes her father's hand, which is how he likes it.

'You're a good girl JJ,' says her mother.

But they can't go out every night and soon the tirades start.

'They're fucking using me. I drag the performance from those bastards. It's in me not them.'

Then that thing snaps in her father's brain and the black dog's in the bedroom with her mother.

Across the tiny landing at the top of the stairs Joss listens to her parents fighting. She lies in her little bed thinking she should do something, help.

When she was little, she'd cried, 'Stop Daddy stop' and only made things worse. Her father had twisted her mother's arm and screamed at her mother that she was turning his daughter against him. Joss doesn't remember those things but she can't make her body move. She thinks she is a bad person.

'You're a fucking slut.'

'Richard I'm sorry. I . . . '

Her father cuts her mother off, 'Oh Alistare.' His voice is high and nasty.

'Richard!'

There is a dull sound and then a small noise escapes on her mother's breath.

'Ow.'

Joss buries her head under her pillow and sings. 'Row row row your boat gently down the stream. Merrily, merrily, merrily, merrily. Life is but a dream.' She sings the song over and over.

Her face gets hot under the pillow and the sheet gets wet from her dribble. She can hardly breathe. She stops singing. It's quiet. Joss takes her head out from under the pillow. Her father snores. She can hear her mother in the kitchen filling the kettle, turning on the stove, getting a cup. Joss hugs her pillow and falls asleep. Thump and cry are woven into her dreams.

On the roof what is grounded becomes light. On the roof Joss can breathe.

Next door is a car park. Behind that is a laundromat. It has a big flat roof. Joss can jump and run on it because no-one can hear her above the grind and hum of the laundromat's machines. Today Joss is a ballerina, she dances on the laundromat roof, above the busy street. She leaps and spins, her arm outstretched, her hands held gracefully, like the dancers in her mother's ballet books. And then she runs with long open strides towards the end of the roof. It is four feet from the corner of the laundromat roof to the corner of her roof. She could walk across the brick fence but it's not the same. She flies.

When she lands, she can feel the smile on her face. Her nose is running. Winter is coming and the wind is cold. She wipes it on the back of her hand. Joss loves being on the roof, away from everything.

Their roof is easy to get onto. All she has to do is climb out her bedroom window and she's on the kitchen roof. The three houses have all had kitchens and bathrooms put on the back. But theirs is the only one where part of the roof has been lifted to let in more light. So Joss has her own rooftop slide.

Joss pulls an old brown school case out her bedroom window and goes to sit in her corner. Her corner is on Judy and Roe's roof. It's the only corner of the roof that's shaded and hidden by branches that have escaped the gardener's eye. Actually, they don't have a gardener. Just Joe with his chainsaw every now and again. Sometimes, in a big wind, a branch falls from one of the gum trees that have grown too big for the garden and her mother has to go and talk to Joe at the milk bar, about borrowing his chainsaw. He never lends it to her mother but comes himself. He always knots a handkerchief and puts it on his head, before slicing the fallen branch like bread. Then he and Joss stack the logs while her mother makes coffee and the three of them sit in the garden and talk. Joe about his home, and her mother about the time she went there, to Malta.

When Joe comes over is one of the few times anyone else but Joss uses the garden. Sometimes, on sunny, Sunday mornings Judy and Roe use it.

They emerge from their back door with coffee and papers. They drag out a couple of chairs and sit in the sun. They talk about getting the garden in order.

When Judy and Roe are in the garden, Joss is very quiet on the roof. She likes watching them, likes the way they talk. She lies there hidden, listening, tasting their life. She listens for the code in the easy slip and slide of their words but there isn't one. And then they disappear, dragging their chairs back inside.

The other thing that happens on Sundays is that her father sticks his nose out the back door and gives a weather report. It's always the same because her father hates Sundays. He opens the back door and stands there for a few minutes and then his words rise and slip over the edge of the leaf-filled guttering where they get stuck.

'Bloody weather. Jesus, this is an ugly fucking city.'

Joss opens her school case and takes out a small drawing pad, some ink and a pen. She sits down and crosses her legs. She is going to draw the ivy climbing up the wall. A picture for her mother. Her mother has been tired today.

Her father is in a good mood when he comes home. It's as though the night before hadn't happened.

'What have my two little mice been doing today, eh? EH? EH?'

He tickles Joss, she giggles and curls like a cat at her father's feet. Joss looks up at her mother but her mother turns away and fixes herself a drink.

Her father rubs his foot across Joss's stomach, he shakes her up. Joss laughs. 'I've got something for you Daddy,' she says. It just comes out, so she runs upstairs and takes the picture from her school case.

When she gives it to her father he picks her up and swings her round. 'My little mouse. What a girl. Look at this. She's fucking brilliant.' Joss doesn't look at her mother she cuddles closer to her Daddy.

'You want Chinese,' he says. Joss nods. 'Come on then lets go!'

At the restaurant her father tells her mother how beautiful she is. He butters her up. By the end of the evening the three of them are laughing and when they get home he tells Joss a bedtime story.

He stands in the middle of her room in a stream of light that comes from the landing. He uses his hands. He is weaving the weather. He brings thunder and lightning into Joss's room.

'The noontide sun, call'd forth the mutinous winds,
And 'twixt the green sea and the azured vault
Set roaring war: to the dread rattling thunder
Have I given fire, and rifted Jove's stout oak
With his own bolt: the strong-based promontory
Have I made shake: and by the spurs pluck'd up
The pine and cedar: graves, at my command,
Have waked their sleepers, oped, and let them forth
By my so potent art.'

Her father is a magic man.

School

'I was born in Ballarat.'

'Me Mum had me at home.'

'You know the big place on the corner? That's where I was born.'

'I thought you had to go to a hospital.'

'Don't think so.'

The little girls' voices bounce off the concrete playground. Joss practises hurdling the tennis net. She doesn't like little girls very much. But her friend is with them, so when she has finished her jumping, sticky and red, she wanders over to join them.

'Where were you born? 'All those plain-faced little girls stare at her, waiting for an answer. They want something from her. Joss can feel it.

'In the middle of the ocean on a boat. I don't come from anywhere.'

'Wow!'

'I've never been on a boat.' The little girls like Joss's story. They chatter, one over another, until Ann's sandflat voice cuts in and she fixes Joss with her shallow blue eyes.

'Sure you were!' Her words have the weight of ringlets and a Barbie doll behind them. The muscles in Joss's belly tighten. She lifts her chin slightly and puts a laugh in her eyes. The kind her father sometimes gets in his. She holds Ann's look.

'My mother had to be fed oysters so she wouldn't lose me,' she says.

'What's an oyster?' asks one of the little girls.

Ann puts her hands on her hips.

'There a kind of shellfish,' says Joss's friend. 'They're what pearls come from.'

'Do you eat the pearls?'

'Course not, stupid,' says Ann.

The bell rings. Joss's friend grabs her by the elbow and drags her towards the grade three classroom. Ann watches them. She gathers nastiness on her tongue.

'She's a liar.' Ann's voice rolls down the convent's concrete covered walkway and hits Joss from behind. Bang. She and her friend keep walking.

Joss sits at the top of the stairs and watches her mother talking to the landlord. She has bought a packet of Tim Tams and made coffee.

'Robert, I feel awful about this but for some reason Richard won't get paid till next week.'

'Don't worry about it, Clair. Next week'll be fine. How's the new wiring holding up?'

'We haven't blown one bulb.' Her mother laughs lightly. 'That a little wire can make all that difference.'

He's a nice man their landlord. Her father doesn't like him because he's got long hair, but Joss and her mother do. They like his girlfriend too. She's all blonde and willowy like grass in summer. She drinks tea without sugar.

She gave Joss a sip once. 'Here, try it,' she'd said, holding out an earthenware cup. Joss had taken the smooth brown cup in her hands and sipped. Her tongue had puckered from the tannin, like a sea anemone when you touch it. But from that day on Joss drank tea without sugar. She wanted to be like the landlord's girlfriend. When she grew up she was going to have earthenware plates and cups. Joss wishes they still lived next-door instead of the small balding man who never smiles.

'Hello, young Jocelyn. I didn't see you up there,' says the landlord, snapping Joss out of her daydream.

'Hello.'

'Aren't you going to have a biscuit?'

Joss bounces down the stairs.

'She's already had three.' Her mother hands her another.

'I'm growing.'

'Good for you,' he says and drains his cup. 'Thanks for the coffee, Clair.'

Her mother sees him to the door. Joss eats the last biscuit. She knows her father was paid this week. She'd watched her mother divide the money into little piles at the dining table. It had taken her a long time because she kept shaking her head and starting again.

'Bye, Robert. Thanks.' Her mother closes the front door. She's left her smile outside. She walks down the tiny hallway biting her lip. Joss follows her.

'Mum?'

Her mother stops and looks at her.

'It's alright,' she says. 'It'll be alright.'

'Maybe we could . . .' Joss doesn't finish the sentence. She doesn't know what they could do.

Her mother smiles. 'Don't worry. We'll think of something.'

Her mother collects Joss from school early the next day. She knocks at the glass door of the grade three classroom and apologizes in whispers to Joss's teacher. Sister Beatrice is not pleased.

When Joss and her mother get outside the school, her

16

mother stops, takes a handkerchief from her handbag and spits on it.

'Hold still,' she says and rubs at Joss's face.

'Where are we going?' asks Joss.

'To the city.'

Joss's mother walks briskly to the tram stop, holding Joss by the wrist. Joss hates it when she does that. They catch a Number 59 tram all the way through the city to the end of Bourke Street.

On the tram her mother takes a scrap of paper out of her handbag, it has an address written on it. She looks at it and sighs. Then she clips her handbag shut, sits up straight and looks determinedly out the window. Joss wants to ask her mother what's going on, where they're going, but she knows she can't.

There's nothing she can do when her mother's in one of these moods, wound tight and ready to snap, except hold everything inside and try not to talk or fidget.

The woman next to Joss gets off the tram. Joss kneels, careful to keep her feet off the seat, and looks out the window too.

People in suits walk fast along the street without smiling. Down near Myer, young girls in pretty clothes weave their way past mothers with pushers, and young men in business suits eat sandwiches without taking them out of their paper bags.

A little boy gets away from his mother, she calls after him to stop. He doesn't. He just turns his head to look at his mother and keeps running, straight into a 'No Standing' sign. Both Joss and her mum flinch. They catch each other's eye and begin to giggle. Her mother's smile breaks into a laugh. It's catching. Being on a crowded city tram just makes it worse. Neither of them can stop laughing. Her mother's eyes fill with tears and she has to put her head between her legs to stop them running down her face and smudging her make-up. That only makes it worse for Joss. She thinks she'll die from laughter. They almost miss their stop. It's just luck that her mother gets it together in time to pull the cord. The tram jerks to a halt and they race across the road holding hands.

Standing on the street corner, her mother blinks and dabs at her eyes with a scrunched-up tissue.

'I'm going to try and get a job,' she says. 'Making sandwiches.'

'Mum, that's fantastic!' Her mother begins to laugh again.

'It's nothing flash, JJ.'

'It's a job.'

'It's money.'

At the sandwich bar Joss slides quietly into a corner booth and watches.

'You can make the sandwich?' says a Yugoslavian woman with dyed red hair sitting in the corner and peering at Joss's mother through the smoke of her cigarette.

'Yes, I can make sandwiches.'

'Show me.'

Her mother puts her handbag down on the counter.

'What would you like?'

'Two ham with mustard, one tomato and cheese and one egg with mayonnaise and onion.'

Her mother walks around the counter.

'Please,' says the woman, rolling the word out with her rich accent before she smiles. Joss wants to hit her. She reminds Joss of an overfed cat.

Her mother gets the job. To celebrate, they have afternoon tea at a coffee lounge in Collins Street.

'I thought she didn't like you,' says Joss.

'I think she's like that with everyone.'

The young waitress brings their order.

'Thank you,' says her mother. Joss spoons the froth off her hot chocolate.

'JJ. This is just between you and me. OK?'

Joss nods. She feels very grown-up. Her mother pours herself a cup of tea and Joss picks all the raisins out of her toast.

Winter

Winter comes, the rent is never late and life in the doll's house settles into a kind of routine.

Every afternoon, Monday to Friday, Joss walks home from school by herself. She buys a chocolate Paddle Pop at Joe's and then climbs over the back fence and lets herself in through the bathroom window. Her mother gave her a front door key the day she got the job, but Joss has lost it. She hasn't told her mother because she prefers climbing in the window. The house seems friendlier if you enter that way.

Her mother is always home by four-fifteen and until then Joss never answers the telephone. Her mother hasn't told her not to. But Joss has watched a lot of films where people pick up phones when they shouldn't. It always gets them into trouble. Joss is smarter than that.

One day there is a tram strike and Joss's mother doesn't get home until quarter past five. She bursts through the front door screaming 'JJ! JJ, where are you!' She looks like a wild thing, her hair tossed around her face, her eyes angry. She grabs Joss by the shoulders and shakes her.

'Why? Why didn't you answer the phone?' her voice is gravel.

'In case it was Daddy.' Her mother stops shaking her then.

Their routine is broken only by the unpredictability of her father's moods. But that in itself is predictable and takes up most of her mother's time. Her mother manages to keep the black dog away most of the winter. She cajoles, takes the insults. He only hits her a few times. Mostly she distracts him. Joss helps by keeping out of the way, unless her Daddy calls her and then she tries to be what he wants her to be. Cuddly and quiet, entertaining, playful. It's always different.

Today her father is melancholy. It's Sunday. Her mother has invited people for lunch and is busy in the kitchen cooking stew with red wine. The house smells rich. It's Joss's job to keep her father happy. She sits on his lap in front of the fire and strokes his moustache.

'Where do you come from Daddy?'

'I don't know.'

'You don't know!'

'No. I was found wrapped in newspaper outside a church in England.'

Joss thinks about the old man in the park. The one she's been throwing money out in the lane for. She's seen him stuffing newspaper down his shirt.

There's a knock at the door. Her father's mood changes.

'Up you pop.' Joss jumps off his lap. 'They're here,' her father calls to the kitchen and her mother comes bustling down the tiny hallway. Joss sits on the stairs and waits.

Uncle Bob gives her father a bottle of wine. Aunty Irene has baked a chocolate cake. Bob and Irene are not really Joss's uncle and aunt. Uncle Bob pushes buttons for her father in the control room, but one day he will own the Company. That's why she's got to call him

Uncle. The Company's one big family, that's what every-one says. From having no uncles or aunts, Joss has suddenly got so many she can't remember their names.

'Ah, just look at how the monster's growing.' Uncle Bob attacks Joss on the stairs. He calls it tickling. Every-one laughs. Joss giggles even though it hurts and she's a bit embarrassed. Uncle Bob gives her one last wallop on the backside and follows the others into the dining room.

Joss sets the table and helps her mother serve. After lunch she asks if she may be excused.

It is a grey day, damp underfoot, with showers of fine rain. It is a day for being on the ground. Joss walks across the little park. She crosses the road and wanders past the milk bar, it's closed. Joss peaks over the side fence Joe's not working on his boat; their yard is deserted and the back door is locked. Joss keeps walking. A group of boys play soccer on the road, Joss turns down the laneway.

She runs her hand along the old wood of the back fences and kicks at the dirt between the cobbled stones. Someone has dumped a lot of cardboard boxes outside their back fence. They're all soggy from the rain. Joss rummages through them. She likes scavenging. But there's nothing, just a heap of old papers and some bottles. At the end of the lane Joss crosses the road and disappears down the lane on the other side. This lane is her favourite. It cuts in behind the houses of the block on funny angles. Joss finds an old pot, a rusted piece of metal, like a tractor-spring, and a puppy.

The puppy looks at her. Joss bends down. The puppy comes. She picks it up and the puppy rests its head on her shoulder. She can feel its little breath, warm on her neck. It makes her heart hurt. She'll give it a home.

When Joss gets back everyone is pissed.

'Aw look at the little thing. Cutesy, cutesy, cutesy.' For one awful minute Joss thinks Aunty Irene's going to kiss the puppy.

'It's shivering. Shouldn't we give it something?'

'I'll get some milk.'

'Put a slug of brandy in it,' says her father. He picks the puppy up and looks at it. Joss holds her breath. Please, please God, she prays inside.

'Obviously the runt. The runt's always the best one out of a litter. And a mongrel too. No vet bills.' Her father looks at her. 'Just like your mother, always bringing home strays.'

'Is that how she got you?' puts in Uncle Bob. He laughs, pleased with his one-liner. Joss reaches up and takes the puppy from her father before he changes his mind.

'Thank you Daddy.' She gives her father the biggest smile she can. He winks at her.

'Very funny, Bob. Don't give up your day job.'

Joss's puppy becomes known as Mischief, Misi for short. She chews holes in Joss's father's socks but is always so pleased to see him that she never really gets into trouble. Misi only has one flaw: she kills chickens.

Trouble

Joss was never really sure what made her do it. Smuggle her dog to school in her bag. But she certainly hadn't been thinking about the nuns' chickens.

'Six! Six!' Sister Beatrice squeals holding up a handful of feathers and shaking them at Joss. 'How could you have done such a thing?'

'It wasn't me Sister. It was my dog.'

'You young lady are a BOLD, BOLD article.' Sister Beatrice pokes Joss in the shoulder with her bony finger. 'BOLD, BOLD.'

A feather floats up in the air between them. Someone in the class giggles. Sister Beatrice spins around, knocking the cheap statue of the Virgin Mary she keeps on her desk. It falls head first and breaks. Sister Beatrice falls to her knees.

'Oh! Oh! Now look what you've done!'

Her mother sits, knees together, back straight, hands resting across her handbag, on the visitor's chair in Mother Superior's office, as she is told the whole ghastly story.

'Mother, I am so sorry. We will of course buy the convent six new chickens.' Her mother bites the inside of her lip to stop herself from laughing. Joss looks at the floor. She can feel the tickle of laughter rising. Her mother says it's the Irish in them. Out of the corner of her eye Joss sees her mother look down and shake her head before she says, 'I don't know what could have got into her.'

When her father arrives home that night he is confronted by Joss and her mother giggling and chasing twelve tiny chickens around the house, while Misi whines at the back door.

'What the . . . !'

The story pours out.

'And the dog is chained behind the nun's alcove,' says Joss, impersonating the Mother Superior.

'Thank you, Mother,' says her mother laughing. They are doing a re-enactment for her father. He laughs.

'Jesus, let the poor dog in. Chained behind the bloody nun's alcove.'

'Father Brannigan didn't think I'd done anything wrong. He gave me a lolly after my confession. He says Sister Beatrice doesn't like children or dogs.'

'Then what the fuck is she doing being a teacher?'

Her father's words have swallowed all the laughter.

'Richard,' her mother says genially, not pleading but appealing.

'Don't Richard me.'

'Daddy please.'

'I'm not going to have my daughter . . . ' Joss stops being there. She falls backwards into herself and gets out of the way.

Her mother steps between her and her father. 'I know it doesn't seem right, Richard, but . . . ' he cuts her off.

Joss gets down on her hands and knees and begins to collect the chickens. By the time she has them all in the cardboard box her mother has stopped saying anything. She just stands in the middle of the room and nods. Joss carries the chickens upstairs to her room and closes the door. But she can still hear him. She sits down on the floor and puts her hand into the box with the chickens. They run underneath her open palm. She could squeeze. She could squeeze really tight.

The trapped chicken cheeps and cheeps. Joss picks it up and cradles it. 'There, there little one it's alright. I'm here.'

The next morning when Joss comes downstairs her mother is already up. She is dressed, has make-up on and is wearing a pair of dark glasses. They are blue with wings. She sits sipping tea at the dining-room table. Joss gets the Coco Pops from the kitchen cupboard, a bowl and a spoon. Her mother comes into the kitchen and gets the milk. She follows Joss back into the dining room. They both sit down. Joss pours herself a bowl of cereal. She concentrates on the first mouthful. It's very sweet.

'Won't it be fun,' says her mother. Joss looks up. Her mother's gone all cutesy. Joss can see purple at the edge of her mother's eye.

'I'm not going to work today. I'll be here when you get home from school.'

Joss carries the chickens to school in the box. All the girls want to pat them. Joss and her friend let them, for two cents each. Sister Beatrice doesn't speak to Joss all day. She just keeps looking at her. Joss pretends she doesn't care. She and her friend buy Twisties at lunchtime.

When Joss gets home the house is shiny clean and her mother is baking. Her hands are dusted in flour. She is making pastry for a pie.

'Nothing like a bit of spit and polish,' she says rolling out the pastry with a milk bottle. She looks at Joss and smiles with her mouth. Her eyes are hidden behind her batwing glasses. Joss smiles with her mouth too and heads for the front door. She calls her dog, 'Come on Misi,' and goes to the park to play.

Hanging upside down from the old elm, Joss sees her mother watching her from the top bedroom window. Her mother isn't smiling. Joss knows her mother wants her to come inside and be with her. She can feel the pull. Joss pretends she hasn't seen her. She jumps down out of the tree and runs further up the park where her mother can't see.

She is a Gypsy girl in an Italian village and her dog can do tricks. Maria opens her front door and sweeps dirt out onto the street. 'Ciao Mama,' calls Joss. Maria doesn't hear her, she slams the door shut. Joss lifts up Misi's front paws and makes her dance. 'Da da da daa dum da dum da dum. Da da da daa dum da dum da dum.' She and Misi roll around on the grass together until the smell of dog poo gets too close. Joss sits up. Misi's excited. She runs in circles chasing her tail.

Down the lane, across the road, Joss sees the old man. He's having a pee. Joss jumps up. She wants to talk to him. She runs across the road, Misi follows. She stops at the corner of the laneway and watches. He shakes his dick and she says, 'Hi.'

He starts and fumbles with his pants.

'Fuuck off.' He slurs. He takes a step forward and makes a noise to frighten her away. She doesn't move.

'Pah. Go away.'

'My Daddy was found wrapped in newspaper.'

'So?'

'Does it keep you warm?'

The old man's spine straightens slightly. He almost smiles.

'Look girlie, you can't talk to me.'

Joss and Misi go into the lane.

The old man bends and strokes the dog.

'Her name's Misi.'

The old man scratches Misi under the chin.

'People wouldn't like you chatting to me.'

'That doesn't matter,' says Joss. The old man laughs. To Joss his laughter sounds like a rough sea, all tumbled with sand.

'Doesn't it?' He spits on the cobbled stones. 'People have bad minds.' The old man shakes his head and turns away.

'It is you who finds the money. Isn't it?' asks Joss.

He stops and looks at her. 'Yeh. But couldn't you put it in a pile. You don't have to throw it round.'

'I never thought of that.'

'No. I guess you wouldn't have.' The old man sniffs. 'Undercover, girlie. Keep it undercover.' He winks at her. Joss raises her hand and sticks up her thumb, 'Thumb to thumb' she says. The old man presses his print to hers.

Ripples

By quarter to seven her father still isn't home and he hasn't phoned. Joss and her mother eat. Her mother picks at her food and moves it round the plate. She doesn't eat much.

At seven-thirty her father comes through the front door. He doesn't look at either Joss or her mother. He doesn't say hello. He walks straight through to the dining room, dumps his stuff on the table and pours himself a drink.

Joss kneels up on the big black armchair so she can see her father in the other room. Her mother tells her to sit down and finish her dinner. On the television, Rolf Harris is playing the washboard and singing 'Tie Me Kangaroo Down Sport'. Joss hears her father pour himself another drink.

She finishes her dinner and carries her plate through to the kitchen. Her father is sitting in the dining room turning his glass around and around in his hand. Joss scrapes the food on her plate into Misi's bowl. She puts her plate in the sink. Her father is pouring himself another drink. Joss doesn't know what to do. Her mother is in the lounge room. Her father is in the dining room. She is in the kitchen and no-one is saying anything.

The phone rings. Her father snatches up the receiver. He usually lets her mother answer it.

'Barry! What can I do you for?' Her father takes a sip of his drink. He has an unfriendly look on his face. Her father says actors always want something from him. Barry is one of her father's actors.

'What meeting?'

Joss watches her father unfold, his brow unknits and his shoulders straighten.

'Too bloody right I'm coming. See you there.' Her father sculls his drink, slams down his glass and picks up his jacket.

'I'm going out. Australian Content meeting. See you later.' He pulls the front door closed behind him. Her father believes he has always been going to that meeting. That's why he'd been sitting in the dining room. He'd been waiting for Barry to ring.

At eight-ten, her mother puts Joss to bed. She scratches her head. Gives her ten pats.

'See you later alligator.'

'In a while crocodile.'

'Night.'

'Night.' Her mother goes downstairs. She turns on the television, *Ironside*. Joss sneaks out onto the landing. She can see the telly from up there. Her mother takes off her dark glasses and puts them on the coffee table. She gingerly touches the side of her head with her fingers. A car stops outside their house. Her mother goes to the window and looks out. Joss knows it's not her father's car. His car rumbles.

'Mum?'

'Oh go to bed JJ.'

At quarter to ten, her mother turns off the television and goes into the bathroom. Joss hears the water pipes clunk as her mother turns on the hot tap. Joss's mother always washes her face the same way. She fills the sink, she cups her hands and then she splashes a little water on her face. When she pats her face dry you notice how long her fingers are.

Joss hears her mother turn off the lights in the kitchen and the dining room. Hears her walk slowly up the stairs. Her parents' bed creaks, Joss feels her mother giving up her weight to the old mattress. Silence. Light from her parents' bedroom shines across the landing and into Joss's room. Joss listens for her father's car.

In the morning when Joss comes downstairs the lamp is on. Joss knows her mother has left it on for her father. Her mother has this thing about always keeping a light burning in the window.

Joss lets Misi out and checks to see if there's any cereal. There's only crumbs. She wonders if he's home.

She goes upstairs and peeks into her parents' bedroom. He's not. Her mother is asleep curled like a ball in the bed. There are crumpled tissues on the floor and a half-drunk cup of tea. Joss tries to imagine her mother sitting up in bed last night. Had she been crying or did she have a runny nose?

Asleep, her mother doesn't look the same. She looks smaller, her features finer. Looking down on her Joss realizes that she doesn't know much about her mother. She knows that she is an actress, that once she was a dancer, that her father thinks her mother has sexy legs. She knows that her mother's mother died two weeks after she was born, that she was brought up by her aunt and that her mother's father never spoke a single word to her although they lived in the same house for eighteen years. He blamed her for her mother's death. Joss didn't know she knew that. She turns and leaves the bedroom. The floorboards creak.

31

On the stairs, Joss wonders about all the spaces in life, the bits she's not around for, where so many things seem to change. People's moods. The furniture. Her mother often rearranges the furniture at night when Joss is sleeping. It makes it weird in the morning, like waking up at the wrong end of the bed.

Her father comes home that afternoon. He is standing in the middle of the kitchen, holding a bunch of flowers, when Joss bounds in the back door. Her mother has been leaning against the stove with her arms folded. When she sees Joss, she reaches out and takes the flowers. She puts them in water. She doesn't take the paper off.

'I'm sorry,' says her father softly.

Her mother has her back to him. 'Where were you?'

Her father turns her mother around. He takes her glasses off and puts them on the kitchen bench. He touches the purple around her eye. He is very gentle. 'Does it hurt?'

'Yes it hurts,' whispers her mother. Her father lifts her mother's chin so she has to look at him. The smell of the roast is all around them. 'You're the best thing that ever happened in my life. You know that, don't you?' He is talking her mother around, Joss can feel it and he's taking up a lot of room. Joss calls Misi and goes upstairs. When he's home, her father wears their house like a coat.

Joss lies on the roof with Misi and watches the sky. A fox changes into an eagle. The eagle is blown apart by the wind and each of its pieces turn into something else.

'JJ! Dinner's ready.'

They eat dinner in front of the telly. Joss chases peas around her plate. The newsreader says Mao Tse-tung and Nixon have made an uneasy peace. Joss looks at her parents.

After dinner her mother clears away the plates. Her

father stays sitting sprawled in the big black armchair, his feet on the table. His show will be on soon. Her mother fixes him a drink. She hands it to him. He doesn't take it. He fingers the big red flowers on her mother's dress.

'I could take a week off,' he says and runs his hand up the back of her mother's leg. Her mother doesn't say anything. She hands him his drink again. He smiles and takes it.

Joss rolls onto her back and closes her eyes. She thinks about gutting fish, the knife pushing against the white underbelly of a black bream. She can see its belly giving, until it is stretched so tight it can give no more and the knife nicks the skin.

Meetings

Joss's father doesn't take a week off work. He never
mentions the idea again. He's busy.

Joss and her mother stand at the kitchen bench cutting
up gravy beef; her mother for their dinner, Joss for the
dog.
    'Will Daddy be home tonight?'
    'No. He's got another meeting.' Her mother throws a
handful of meat into the pot. Joss slices along a line of
white sinew.
    'They must have a lot to talk about,' she says and looks
at her mother out of the corner of her eye.
    'Always,' says her mother. Joss giggles.
    Joss and her mother would never say so, but it is easier
when he is out a lot and they are left to themselves. It
isn't that they do much together. Mostly they just let each
other be, except on Friday nights when they play poker
for Minties.

August is grey and cold following July without change.
Joss finds a warm spot on the laundromat roof where
the hot air from the dryers comes rushing out. She builds
a shelter over the vent, cardboard boxes covered in plastic; a little house. Joss finds the old man in the park. She
takes him to the alley behind her house and shows him

how to climb up onto the laundromat roof. She does it three times to show him how easy it is but he just stands in the laneway shaking his head.

'Come on! It's easy!'

'What do you want me to do? Break me bloody neck!'

'It's easy!'

'Huh!' The old man spits.

'Huh to you too!' Joss spits down into the laneway. She turns and storms across the laundromat roof. She jumps down into the tall boy's—Timmy's—backyard. She knocks on his back door. No-one answers. Joss goes and takes the big ladder from the shed anyway. He hasn't been using it much lately. She'll ask him later.

Joss leans the ladder up against the brick fence and climbs back onto the laundromat roof. She drags the ladder up after her. It scrapes as she drags it across the roof. She lowers it down into the laneway on the other side of the laundromat.

The old man has gone.

'Stupid old bugger,' says Joss to the grey drizzle. She leaves the ladder.

Joss wakes. Her parents are fighting. Her body's warm. Her face is cool. The window's open. It's her mother fighting.

'How many meetings can you have in one week?' Her mother's voice is cheap and high like nylon ripping.

'You're crazy, you know that!'

'Crazy! I'll show you crazy!' Glass shatters against stone.

'Jesus Fucking Christ.' There's a laugh in her father's voice.

'Don't,' says her father. 'I'm tired.'

Joss hears him on the stairs and then her mother begins to cry. Joss closes her eyes and imagines herself away.

The next day at school, Joss gets into trouble for not having a blazer. They have to wave flags and sing when the Queen drives by. Joss borrows a blazer and the Queen is late. Six hundred children stand for an hour and a half in the freezing wind, waiting.

'My Dad thinks my Mum's crazy,' whispers Joss to her friend.

'My Mum thinks my sister's crazy.'

'Really?'

Her friend nods. Joss pulls up her socks.

Joss begins to miss her father. She forgets the bad things. She wants a bedtime story and a cuddle. She wants to laugh, be tickled and have a pillow-fight.

On Saturday morning her father is home. Asleep upstairs. 'Don't wake your father,' says her mother. 'He's very tired.'

Joss goes upstairs and crawls into bed beside him. She wraps one arm around his chest and curls around him, spoon to spoon. She is a little spoon and he is a big spoon; the fit is not quite right. He begins to stir, rolls over and opens his eyes. Joss sits up and crosses her legs.

'Good morning, Daddy.'

'Umm. My little mouse, good morning.'

'Daddy can we go fishing today? Well it's not really fishing but it sort of is. One of the girls at school said there were yabbies in the lake in the park and that you can . . . ' Joss doesn't think she talks a lot. It always surprises her when her school report says, 'If Jocelyn would talk less and work more, she would be an excellent student'.

'Alright, alright; but later.'

Joss is so excited she ignores the distance between her parents, the cool. Her mother makes her father breakfast. Her father reads the paper. Her mother puts on a record.

Her father says he can't think with that racket. Her mother goes to shower. Her father tells her to be quick; he wants a bath. Joss says she has some bubbles he can use. He pats her head.

At eleven he goes out. He's got some business. Joss goes and sits on the roof and rips the flesh from the veins of leaves.

Joss's father sticks his head out her bedroom window. 'Well come on. Are we going or what?' To Joss, his smile is like the fizz in a sherbet bomb, POW, your mouth is alive. But with him, everything comes to life.

She follows him, like an eager puppy, as he moves through the house rummaging in the cupboard under the stairs for buckets and in the kitchen drawers for string. He takes chops from the fridge for bait. Joss takes whatever he hands her. Her mother sits in the dining room, polishing silver. She doesn't say a word.

'Bye Mummy,' calls Joss as her father shepherds her out the front door. The door slams behind them.

They walk the three blocks to the Exhibition Gardens, buckets and string tangling around them. Her father is in a good mood. An old Greek man calls from his front porch. 'They are good. Sweet.' Her father waves, 'Too right, mate.' It's magic. Everything looks different to Joss. The old houses look beautiful and the streets don't feel deserted.

It doesn't matter that the ground is damp. They take off their shoes and dangle their feet in the brown, icy water. When Joss feels a tug on her string her father scoops the green, nipping shellfish from the water in a net he has made from one of her mother's stockings and a coat-hanger. He tells Joss about the mud crabs in Western Australia.

'They're three feet wide, nippers that could rip your arm off. And they'll bloody chase you if you give them half a chance. Finding a pot big enough to cook them in, that was the problem!'

'What did you do?'

'Forty-four gallon drum. Cooked them on the beach. Beautiful. The food of Gods.' Joss dangles a piece of meat into the bucket with the yabbies. A big one tugs at it and pulls it from her fingers.

When they get home, her father throws the yabbies into a pot of boiling water. They claw and scrape at the sides of the pot. Joss never thought they'd do that. Her father pushes them back in and sticks a lid on. Joss runs outside into the woodshed. She shakes her hands and head. She can feel the boiling water against her skin. She's going to be sick. She just killed all those yabbies. Boiled them alive.

At dinnertime she cannot eat them. Her father is angry.

'What do you mean you can't eat them? You wanted to go fishing. When I was your age I'd have given anything to have a meal like this. Well?'

Joss looks up at her father. She doesn't want him to be angry with her, but she can still feel the water.

'They're different from fish.'

Her father's lip curls like an angry dog. He leans across the table and hits her with an open hand.

'Richard don't! She didn't know.' Her mother has him by the arm. He throws her mother back against the wall and stands over her.

'Don't ever take her side against me! Do you understand?'

Her mother nods. He looks at Joss, 'Get to your room.'

Joss slides off her chair. At the foot of the stairs she pats the side of her leg to call Misi.

'Leave the dog here.' He's not even looking at her.

Joss goes upstairs. She closes her bedroom door. Her room is cold. She climbs into bed with her clothes on.

She lies there listening but there is no sound in the house, no talking, no movement. It is as if the house has died. Joss tries not to let her mind wander because it will wander to bad things and she's scared.

Just as the bed begins to warm up Joss needs to go to the toilet. She can't go downstairs. Joss hangs her bottom out her bedroom window and pisses on the roof. It sounds like heavy rain.

As she climbs back into bed she hears her parents. They have started talking, quiet, disjointed. She can't hear what they're saying but at least she knows they're there. In her mind Joss fits the bottom and the top of the house back together. It's not so scary anymore, she just feels bad. She's sorry that she made her Daddy angry. She opens her bedroom door to go downstairs and tell him. Her mother's voice rises in a wail. Joss stops at the top of the stairs.

'What do you think this is? A motel. This isn't easy for me.'

'Nothing's easy for you. Well it's not easy for me either. Having to come home and look at your righteous, bloody face. Miss bloody martyr. You're as sour as the nuns who raised you.' Her mother begins to cry.

'Very touching.'

Her mother stops crying.

There is a long silence. Joss hears her father fix himself a drink, small sounds. She can feel her heart beating in her chest. Her mother's voice is flat when she speaks, like a sea before a big wave comes, 'Are you going to see her again?'

'What do you think?'

Joss steps back into her bedroom and closes the door. She doesn't understand what it is they're arguing about, but she knows it's her fault. She caused it.

In the morning Joss finds her mother sitting at the

dining-room table. Her father has gone. Joss thinks he's gone for good. But her mother says he just had an early call, that everything will be alright. Joss says she's sorry. Her mother tells her not to be silly and to get ready for school.

Holy Water

After that night, her mother changes. She still does everything but her eyes are dull. When her father's home he
acts as though nothing has happened. He teases Joss a
little about the yabbies, all in good fun. But it makes
Joss's stomach tight. She's scared she'll say the wrong
thing, make him angry. So she never asks her mother
anything when her father's home. She always asks him.
Even though she knows he'll say, 'How the hell would
I know. Ask your mother.'

Her mother stops going to work at the sandwich bar
and when the rent is due she just tells Joss's father there
isn't enough money.

'Why the fuck not?'

'Because you've spent it,' she says without looking up
from stringing beans. He hits her, knocking the bowl of
beans onto the ground and storms out. Joss helps her
mother pick up the beans. Her mother doesn't cry.

Joss works out how to get the old man onto the roof. She
puts a bottle of wine at the top of the ladder. The next
day she sees him crawling on his hands and knees across
the laundromat roof to the little shelter, pushing the
bottle of wine in front of him.

Joss tries to cheer her mother up. She makes her cups

of tea and suggests that they do things together. Like take Misi for a walk on a lead, which is something Joss hates doing. Or go for a tram ride down to the sea. Joss knows her mother likes the sea because she always says 'Ah the sea!' whenever anyone mentions the beach. But nothing works. Her mother doesn't even laugh at *Here's Lucy*.

Joss mops up the sauce from her baked beans with a slice of toast. The ABC news has just finished. Her mother stands up and butts her cigarette out. 'Go and get your coat, JJ,' she says.

Outside it is cold and wet. There is no moon. It is a black night, making the streetlights seem very bright and yellow. Her mother is walking with purpose.

'Where are we going?'

'To a meeting.'

Inside the Anglers Hall, three blocks away, are lots of people Joss recognizes; actors, directors and all her uncles. Joss and her mother slip in quietly. No-one notices them because they're all talking at once; all two hundred of them. Joss climbs up on a table so she can see. Her father is standing in the middle of the hall, one leg on a chair—just like in the picture of him as Hamlet she has in her room.

'Look Mummy, it's Daddy!' Her mother nods at Joss and puts her finger to her lips, telling Joss to be quiet. Her mother looks stretched and tense.

'Nowhere,' Joss's father's voice booms out, the crowd quietens. Joss watches her father.

'Nowhere in the world do actors work under the kind of conditions we work under in this country.'

'Or the kind of pay!'

'What fuckin' pay!' Comments fly. Her father waits for them to quieten.

'It's time to change these things. The few shows we have on prime-time television out-rate the cast-off American trash the networks love because they're so fucking cheap.'

'And British trash, you die-hard Pommie!' calls Barry. Everyone laughs.

'Thank you, Barry. And British trash. My point is, if it rates and it does, then this is not just our fight as writers, actors, directors and producers. It is our fight as Australians. It is the fight for an Australian voice.'

The hall erupts with applause. Joss has never heard her father talk like that before, about something bigger than himself. An Australian voice! She's not sure what it means but it sounds important. Joss climbs down off the table and squeezes between the two people in front of her. She's going to tell her father how good his speech was. Her mother grabs her by the wrist.

'We'll wait for him outside.'

Joss has no idea what's going on, but something is. The tone in her mother's voice says she will not be disobeyed.

Joss waits with her mother on the other side of the street. People spill out of the hall. Finally her father emerges with Barry and Uncle Bob. Joss steps forward, her mother's grip tightens. She waits.

'Do you think we can do it? I mean this Liberal government. They hate the Arts.' Barry's voice carries across the road strong and clear on the cool night air.

'Yeh, but the bottom line is . . .'

A bloke pats Uncle Bob on the back as he passes, 'See you mate.'

'. . . See you. That this is not a Liberal country. Take a look.'

Joss watches her father. He doesn't seem interested in Barry and Uncle Bob's conversation. He leans back against the hall, shoves his hands into his pockets and looks up at the sky.

A woman with very blonde hair comes out of the hall and joins them. Her father straightens. The woman slips herself under Barry's arm, between Barry and her father.

'Oh God,' she says. 'Richard, you make me believe it's possible.'

Joss's father smiles. 'Who's for a drink?' he says.

The woman slips her arm through Joss's father's arm. Joss doesn't like that. Uncle Bob says he's out, but Barry wanders off with them down the street.

Her mother's grip has loosened but Joss doesn't want to go to her father anymore. She looks at her mother. Her mother tries to smile. They walk home holding hands.

The next day Joss finds the old man on the laundromat roof.

'Can't bloody get down,' he says.

Joss wants to talk but she shows him how to climb down backwards first. He slips a little but he makes it.

'Rather be cold,' he mutters as he shuffles off down the laneway. Joss follows him.

'You're like a little yapping terrier,' he says pulling a bottle from his coat pocket. It's empty. Disgusted, the old man throws the bottle away.

'Me Mum's sad,' says Joss.

'A lot of people are sad.' The old man's irritated. He needs a drink.

'But she's my mother.'

'Oaw, I don't know what you do. I've never been good with women.' The old man begins to scratch and shuffle from foot to foot. Joss lets him wander off on his own.

She knows he's a dero, knows what that means. But when she has to write a story at school, entitled 'My Best Friend', she writes about the old man. How he lives in the back alleys and scavenges for his food. That he doesn't like people but he likes her. In the story she says he is a cat. She remembers what he said about staying undercover.

Joss has a dream. She is in a house by the sea. Uncle Bob and Aunty Irene are there. Her father is there. All the adults are very tall. Joss wanders through the rambling house looking for her mother. She can't find her. She finds her dog on the mat by the front door. A taxi pulls up and a woman gets out. Her father opens the door and tells Joss it's her mother. The woman has no face. She is dressed in black.

'That's not my mother,' says Joss.

Her father laughs, 'Oh yes it is. Help her with her bags.'

Joss wakes. Her pillow's wet. She's been crying. Misi's whining. She sits up. Her bedroom's filled with shadows.

Hardly a week goes by at Joss's school when there is not a Feast day mass. Joss isn't sure whose Feast day it is today, she isn't feeling very well. She kneels on the velvet crimson board in front of the altar.

'The body and blood of Christ.'

'Amen,' she says.

The priest dunks the wafer of bread into the goblet of wine. Joss sticks out her tongue. The taste of sweet rotting grapes fills her mouth. She gets up and runs from the church. The side door slams shut behind her and she is sick on the asphalt. Joss's stomach contracts again. She is doubled over. She hears little horrified gasps from someone coming up behind her. Through eyes filled with water she sees the old nun's shiny shoes, sticking out beneath the hem of her habit, before she feels the walking-stick come down across her back.

'That is the Body of Christ! The body of Our Lord!'

Joss blinks. The host is lying in a pile of sick dissolving into the black bitumen. Joss's stomach contracts again.

'Pick it up! Pick it up!' cries the old nun bringing her walking-stick down across Joss's back again as she is sick. Someone runs from the chapel and restrains the old nun. Joss cannot stop. Her stomach is pushing all the food out.

'She must make confession, receive absolution!' The old nun is distressed.

'She will Mother, she will.' The young woman calms the old nun and leads her away.

Joss does not make her confession or receive absolution. She spends most of the day in the sick bay and when she gets home she feels the devil strong inside her. She pours half her father's brandy into an empty lemonade bottle. She tops up her father's brandy with water. It still tastes strong to her.

The old man is sitting on the park bench. He has his eyes shut. Joss sits down beside him. He knows it's her. She slips him the bottle.

He opens one eye. A smile slides across his face. He puts the bottle into the pocket of his coat and tries to think of something to say. Joss swings her legs and waits.

'That tall black girl's back,' he says.

'Timmy's girl?'

'Yeah.'

Joss thinks about this for a minute.

'Guess he'll be wanting his ladder back.'

'Well he can't have it.'

'Why not?'

'Someone nicked it.'

'Oh.'

The old man snarls. 'I hate that old bastard. He stole me port.'

Joss looks up. On the other side of the street, coming

46

out of the lane by the milk bar is an old man, shaking his fist and swearing at the sky.

Two days later Timmy comes to their front door and asks Joss's mother if she's seen his ladder. Joss doesn't say anything.

'I guess I'll just have to buy a new one,' he says. Her mother shrugs. 'She's come back,' he says shyly.

'Oh Tim,' says her mother and hugs him.

On Sunday Joss's mother says they're going to mass. She tells Joss to put on her communion dress and her patent leather shoes but Joss's feet have grown and when her mother sees how tight they are she won't let her wear them. She makes her wear her school shoes instead and they walk all the way to Saint Pat's in the city. Before they go in through the big carved doors her mother stops and takes two lace scarves from her handbag. She puts the white one over Joss's head. She wears the black one.

It's a beautiful mass. In Latin. There's singing and young boys, wearing white, swing carved golden incense burners and fill the church with smoke and scent. Joss thinks it's frankincense and myrrh, like the wise men gave to the baby Jesus.

After mass she and her mother light candles in front of a statue of the Virgin Mary. Joss makes a prayer. She says she is sorry she made things bad between her parents, that she didn't mean to. And that if the Virgin Mary could see a way to help she would really appreciate it. When they leave the church Joss dips both hands in the holy water because she likes the smell of it.

When they get home her father has gone out. Joss goes to bed at seven-thirty. He's still not back.

In the morning when Joss gets up the lamp is on in the lounge room. Her father didn't come home. Her mother makes herself a cup of tea and sits at the dining-room table. She doesn't drink it. She just looks at it. Joss goes to school. At lunchtime Ann hits Joss in the head with a tennis ball. She says it was an accident. Joss knows it wasn't.

Her father comes home that night at about five but the only thing he says to her mother is that he's sick of eating sausages. On Tuesday morning he kicks the dog. Joss figures she mustn't have prayed hard enough. That praying must be like flying. You have to believe without a hint of doubt. Wanting is not enough.

September

September winds blow away the grey and the sun rises, yellow, into a blue sky.

Outside Joss feels the spring. In the doll's house it is still winter. She and Misi scavenge in the lanes. Joss picks flowers from honeysuckle bushes that hang over people's back fences. The liquid is watery and not very sweet, weak, like the sunshine.

When Maria goes out, Joss climbs over her back fence and steals three mandarins from a tree in her backyard. She looks for the old man. She wants to give him one but she can't find him. So she goes inside and gives one to her mother.

Her mother is in the bathroom, on her knees leaning over the bathtub, scrubbing. She has rubber gloves on and they're covered in Ajax so Joss peels a mandarin for her. It's a bit green.

'Here Mum.' She pops a piece into her mother's mouth. Her mother makes a face.

'Bitter?'

Her mother nods. Joss pops a piece into her own mouth. Her tongue puckers. Her mother puts one hand on the side of the bath and stands up. Joss thinks she's going to rinse the bath out now. But she doesn't. She starts scrubbing the tiles on the wall around the bath. They don't look dirty to Joss.

Joss picks up the spare Wettex and the Ajax from the bathroom floor. She walks over to the basin and shakes some Ajax into the sink. Where the sink has water on it the Ajax turns blue.

Joss wonders about germs. She pushes some Ajax down into the plughole.

'I know how to make a vaccine, Mum.'

Her mother doesn't say anything.

'I mean if there was an epidemic or something.' Joss shakes some more Ajax into the sink. 'You know, like the black plague.' She looks at her mother.

'That's nice, dear.'

'Do you want me to tell you?'

Her mother turns on the shower to rinse the Ajax off the walls. It runs down into the bath. Joss decides to tell her anyway.

'Just say you'd been sick from something. And then you got better. But everyone else was still sick from it. I'd take a pint of your blood because you'd be a recovered victim. And then I'd put your blood in a jar and tie a rope around the jar and swing it around my head for twenty minutes.'

Her mother turns the shower off and stretches.

'When you stop swinging it around it's all separated. There's three layers.'

Her mother turns around and lifts up the toilet seat.

'But it's only the top one you need. It's clear and it's the vaccine. And then you just give it to people.'

Her mother looks at her and smiles. Joss knows she's trying to think of something to say.

'Where did you learn that?'

'I read it in a book.'

'Pass the Ajax, honey.'

50

Joss passes it to her. Her mother takes the long brush and starts to scrub the toilet.

That night Joss walks up to the takeaway Chinese restaurant with Misi. She orders Sweet and Sour Pork and Fried Rice. Her mother doesn't feel like cooking. She says she's not hungry, but she says Joss has to eat.

When Joss gets home her mother is sitting in front of the telly, knitting. One pearl, one plain, one pearl. Her hands do it all by themselves.

The next day is Sunday. Her father is still not home and her mother stays in bed. Joss watches cartoons and eats Coco Pops.

At nine-thirty, Joss puts on her communion dress and takes twenty cents from her mother's purse. She walks up to the church at the end of the park. It isn't a Catholic church. Joss doesn't know what it is, but old women, dressed in black, sell almonds covered in pale coloured candy and wrapped in little squares of pink or white net, outside. Joss buys one and walks back home through the park. She has squeezed her feet into her old patent leather shoes because they match her dress but as soon as she crosses the road to the park, she takes them off. Her mother was right. They are too small now. The grass is cold and wet with dew. Joss wiggles her toes and leaves her shoes under a tree for someone to find.

She has eaten three of the almonds by the time she gets home. Her mother's still not up. Joss eats the last two almonds. She makes an angel out of the little square of net and leaves it on the dining-room table. Joss goes upstairs and peeks into her parents bedroom. Her mother is awake, looking at the ceiling.

Joss climbs out onto the roof. It's wet with dew like the grass. She scrambles up her rooftop slide. It's good that she has strong hands. The roof is slippery. She slides down fast. Misi barks at her from the window. Joss drags the dog out onto the roof. She hears her mother get up and go downstairs. She scrambles up again. This time it's not as fast because her dress has soaked up all the water. Next time she slides closer to the edge where the dew still beads the tin. The guttering on this part of the roof has not been finished properly. Joss doesn't notice. She slides fast. Sharp metal slices her heel, impaling her, three feet from the bottom of her slide and twenty feet above the ground.

She is brave. She does not cry. She tries to hold herself against the roof so she can lift her foot off the metal spike, but her hands slip. Awkwardly, she dries two patches with the skirt of her dress and pushes her palms hard against the roof, so they can grip against the smooth corrugations. Joss has big hands, too big for a child. She holds herself and lifts her leg. When her foot is free the blood pumps out with the rhythm of her heart. It is dark blood from deep inside. She lets herself slide down, her white dress soaking up the blood that runs in little rivers down the corrugations.

Misi whines and tries to lick her foot. Joss pushes her away and hops to her window. She sits on the sill and calls.

'Mum! Mum!' Joss holds her foot by the ankle. It's bleeding everywhere.

'Mum!' She smells roast lamb. Someone is cooking Sunday lunch. 'Mum!' Joss wonders about warriors. They roast whole lambs on spits and there's always blood.

'What is it?' Her mother is calling from the bottom of the stairs. Joss waits till she comes up. She watches her blood drip onto the roof. It falls with weight, not like water. She tastes it. Her mother comes to the door.

'What is it?' Her mother looks tired and grey, she is wearing an old pair of slacks and her batwing glasses.

'I think you better get a towel, Mum.'

'Oh my God!' Her mother turns white. She crouches to stop herself from being sick, 'My baby.'

Joss swings her legs in her bedroom window and hops down onto her good foot. Her heel is beginning to throb. There's an old T-shirt on the floor of her room. Joss wraps it around her foot.

'It's alright Mum, really.'

Her mother wipes the tears from her eyes. It's the first time Joss has seen her cry all winter. 'Oh! I'm sorry.'

'That's OK. But I think it needs stitches.' Joss slides down the stairs on her bottom. Her mother phones a taxi.

At the doctor's surgery her mother tells the doctor she can feel the injury as though it were her own. The doctor suggests she have a cup of tea and wait outside.

Joss is very brave but when the needle pierces her open flesh she screams and then she cries and cries and cries. A fat nurse holds her down.

Leaving

'Fourteen stitches, eh?' says her father when he comes home. He tweaks her nose and sits on the edge of her bed. Joss doesn't say anything. He asks if he can see her foot. She says no, it's too sore. He tells her about the car accident he and her mother had. He says they all have scars now.

Joss wants to ask him why he doesn't need them, her and her mother, anymore.

Her mother comes in with toast and vegi and a cup of tea with sugar. She slides the tray across Joss's lap and looks at Joss's father. Her cheeks are red and her eyes are angry. He gets up and Joss's mother sits down. She reaches out and brushes the hair back off Joss's face.

'I'm sorry honey. It won't happen again.' She kisses Joss. Her lips are warm. Joss smiles. When she looks up her father has gone.

The next day, Joss works out what she can and can't do with fourteen stitches in her heel. Hopping's OK, around the house. And the stairs are easy. She slides down them on her bottom and crawls up them on her knees. She can manage to climb out onto the roof. But she can't hop on the roof; she has to slide across it on her bottom. Outside, hopping is no good, unless she just wants to cross the

54

road to the park and sit on the grass. But if she wants to go anywhere, to the milk bar or up the street, hopping takes too long, makes her good leg ache and her stitches throb. Joss goes back inside and crawls up the stairs. She rummages under her bed, looking for her roller-skates. She spends the afternoon practising with one skate. It's faster than hopping. The only tricky bit is stopping.

Joss's father comes home at seven. He asks what's for dinner. Joss's mother tells him she and Joss have already eaten and that if he wants something he'd better make it himself. Her father leaves the little house, slamming the door behind him. Her mother picks up Joss's half-eaten bowl of ice-cream and takes it to the kitchen. Joss hadn't actually finished.

Her father doesn't come back home that night. The next day Joss's mother goes out and Joss practises her roller-skating. When her mother comes home, she tells Joss they're going on a holiday. To Sydney. On the train.

Joss hears her father come home late. He stumbles in the front door. The water pipes clunk in the bathroom, where her mother is. The needle scratches across a record. Frank Sinatra's 'The girl from Ipanema' fills the house.

Her father begins to sing. Joss hears the clunk of a bottle against a glass. Her mother's on the stairs.

'Hello to you too!' Her father's in a nasty mood.

Her mother keeps walking up the stairs. Joss catches a glimpse of her on the landing. Her parents' bed creaks. Her father turns up the music. Her mother turns off the light. Joss lies in her bed, wide awake, listening, waiting. But nothing happens. Her father drinks himself to sleep.

Standing at the front door, a roller-skate on her good foot, Misi in an old carpetbag beside her, watching her mother do a last-minute check of the house in case they have forgotten anything, Joss feels guilty.

The railway station smells of people's lives, like the laundromat. Ash and food and dreams all mixed together. Joss and her mother hurry down the platform to sleeping car Number 19.

Misi begins to whine. 'Shush, Misi. Shush' says her mother.

'Give her a pat Mum. She's scared.' Joss skates over. Her mother turns her back on the train and the conductor waiting outside car 19. Joss sticks her hand in the bag.

'It's OK Misi. It's OK.' Misi licks Joss's hand and stops trying to stand up.

The conductor takes their tickets.

'Sleeper 24C. I'll take your bag for you?'

'Oh no, that's fine. Thank you,' says her mother. The conductor shrugs and heads off down the tiny corridor that runs between the berths. Joss and her mother follow.

'These are the ladies' showers, on the right here. They get pretty crowded from about seven tomorrow morning. So you might prefer to freshen up tonight.'

'Thank you. I'll keep that in mind.'

'And this is you here. 24C.'

'Oh wow,' says Joss as she swings herself through the tiny doorway.

'You're pretty good on one roller-skate. Don't know how you'll go once the train's moving though.'

'She'll hop,' says her mother. Joss raises her eyebrows.

'This is your sink and this is your toilet. You just press these two buttons.'

'Where are the beds?'

'The chairs fold out.'

'Can we?'

'Not now Joss.' Her mother's getting nervous about Misi.

'Sorry.'

'Thank you very much for all your help.'

'Not a problem. If you need me. I'm down the hall.' He shuts the door behind him.

'JJ really.'

'Can we pull a bed out?'

'No! We can shut the blinds so we can let your poor dog out.'

Lying in the top bunk, starched white sheets and woollen blankets tucked tight around her, watching the shape of the country race by in silhouette, Joss is happy.

Sydney

No-one meets them at the train station.

'Didn't you call Aurora?' asks Joss. Aurora is Joss's mother's best friend and she lives in Sydney.

'We'll get settled first.' The look in her mother's eye dares Joss to object.

Walking up and down the hills of Sydney with Misi on a lead and Joss on one roller-skate proves very difficult. Her mother hails a cab. The taxidriver suggests places where Joss and her mother might find a room. They all turn Joss's mother away because of the dog. Finally her mother tells the taxidriver to take them to the actors' pub in Elizabeth Street. They get a room there. The publican says if they use the backstairs he won't see the dog and he can't object to what he can't see.

Her mother lugs their cases up the old wooden stairs at the back of the pub. 'It's only for a couple of days,' she says. 'Tomorrow I'll get a job and find us something better.' Joss stops at the top of the stairs. She looks out across the city roofs. Sydney feels different to Melbourne. The streets are narrower and dirtier, the light is different and she can smell the sea.

Children aren't allowed in the pub so her mother

orders two counter dinners and they eat out on the back-stairs with Misi.

Her mother doesn't find a job, but the publican says he has a friend who needs someone to look after his house for a couple of weeks, so they move. It's a tiny old weatherboard house right on the water. Joss likes the boats, the peeling paint on the house, the rambling garden and the crooked outside toilet. It's much better than the pub. At night there are no drunken voices. There is only the sound of the water.

The day after they move her mother calls Aurora. She comes straight over. She arrives with a flourish. Aurora is an actress. She fusses over Joss's mother and talks about getting her back into the business.

'You should never have stopped working you know, darling. It's the downfall of every good actress. Giving one's career up for a man. Even that man. I warned you.'

'You adore Richard, Aurora.'

'That's not the point. I don't have to live with him.'

Joss forgets her mother was an actress. She can't imagine her on a stage. She knows her mother made a film once. Joss had been very young then. She remembers her mother going away and her father looking after her. He was in a bad mood the whole time. He cut the bread for Joss's sandwiches so thick she couldn't get them into her mouth. And he forgot to tell her to put on her underpants before she went to school. She hadn't been able to play on the monkey bars. That was the only time Joss remembered her mother acting.

'Was Mum a good actress?' Joss asks Aurora.

'Good! Clair what are you teaching the girl? She's going to grow up with a completely twisted set of values.'

Her mother laughs.

'She was brilliant. And you, young lady, should remember. You spent most of your first four years in rehearsal rooms and at radio stations.'

'Did I?'

'Oh my God, get me a scotch. There was never any need for your mother to stop working. If it hadn't been for that man she'd have been a star.' Aurora says 'that man' so tenderly, Joss wants to hug her. People she doesn't like are always telling her how lucky she is to have a father like Richard but they don't know and Joss isn't even sure they like him. It's all talk. But with Aurora it isn't talk, she knows.

Joss makes Aurora and her mother butterfly cakes to have with their scotch and Aurora teaches Joss 'a couple of old numbers from the Tiv.' The three of them sing and Aurora does a little soft-shoe. Finally Joss crawls into bed and falls asleep listening to the soft laughter of her mother and Aurora.

A scream wakes Joss. It's dark. The scream is coming from outside. It's her mother. Joss scrambles from her bed and hop–runs out the back door, grabbing a bottle from the kitchen table as she passes. The back door flies open, 'Mum!' Joss has the bottle raised above her head.

'WOOF.'

Joss stops. Her mother is pinned to the toilet wall by a large dog.

'WOOF.' He licks her mother's face.

'He likes you Mum.'

'I don't care! Get him off me!'

Joss's foot heals quickly. The stitches begin to itch. Joss knows they've got to come out. The doctor said ten days. She goes to her mother's make-up bag and takes out a pair of nail scissors. She sits cross-legged on the grass outside and cuts each stitch before pulling it out with a pair of tweezers. When she presses around the scar her heel feels numb. Joss thinks her foot will be tougher now. In summer when she steps on stones it won't hurt so much.

Life with just Joss and her mother is easy. There's a lot of time. They go for walks on the beach. Her mother reads. Joss draws. They eat when they feel like it. Her mother worries about money but she's always done that.

Aurora invites them to come into town for the day. They'll be ladies she says, and window-shop. They have sandwiches at the Rocks and then walk up to the actors' pub.

'Just one quick drink with a few old mates,' says Aurora. 'And you be a good girl. Sit outside and I'll bring you a raspberry lemonade.' Her mother and Aurora disappear into the lounge. Joss kneels up on the seat outside and looks in through the window. Her father is standing by the bar, a single red rose in his hand. He and her mother just look at one another. Aurora orders a lemonade and a scotch, she carries them through the lounge as though nothing were going on. She comes outside and sits down next to Joss.

'Come on. Give them a bit of privacy.' Joss turns around and sits down. She takes the lemonade and sips but she can't taste it. Her heart is beating too hard.

Her mother hadn't actually told Joss they were leaving her father. But Joss had known. And now nobody tells Joss they're going home. Her father simply comes out of the pub, sweeps her up in his arms and says, 'How about oysters for dinner?'

They spend two more days in Sydney with her father

showing them 'his town' and then they fly home. Misi is drugged and put in a cage. Joss says she would rather have gone by train. Her parents laugh. Joss doesn't think it's funny.

Home

As soon as Joss gets home she climbs out onto the roof. Her mother yells from the back door for her to put her shoes on. Joss yells down that she's already got them on and walks across the wall to the laundromat roof. She misses the sea, the green lawn and rambling garden of the weatherboard cottage. She lies on her belly and looks out over Elgin Street. Some kids chase their father up the street.

'Dad!'

'Wait up!'

'Aw Dad, wait!' Their father doesn't wait and the kids have to run to keep up. Joss watches them disappear around the corner.

When Joss gets back to school Sister Beatrice frowns. 'Gallivanting,' she says, 'will do little for your education Jocelyn. No matter what your mother thinks.'

There is also a new girl, Sylvie Gorgon. Sylvie is plain with neat hair and no imagination. For some reason Joss cannot work out, her friend seems to have taken to her.

After four lunch hours spent trying to be polite Joss has had enough. She tells her friend she has to choose who she's going to be friends with. Joss's friend tells her not to be stupid. Joss stands and confronts the two girls, heat rising to her cheeks.

'It's her or me. You can't have it both ways.'

'And you can't tell me who I'm going to be friends with.'

'Well?'

'You're just jealous.'

'And you're just stupid.' Joss turns and walks away.

She hides all afternoon in the girls' toilet. It hurts. She wants to hit and punch and scream. She doesn't want to see anyone. Joss leaves the school just before the bell rings. When she gets home she goes to her room and locks the door. The next day Joss refuses to go to school.

On the weekend her mother and father want to play happy families. They drag Joss off to Victoria Market on Saturday morning and buy lots of food. Her mother bakes all afternoon and her father wants her to watch the footy with him.

'Did you see that mark? The man's a legend.' Joss cuts herself another slice of chocolate cake. She thinks her parents are stupid too.

On Sunday her father tries to trick himself. He wakes them all at four in the morning and drives to Echuca. But eight o'clock on a Sunday morning in Echuca is the same as eight o'clock on a Sunday morning anywhere in Australia. Nothing's open and the quiet of Sunday hangs all around you.

Her father slams the car door. The sound rolls down the empty street. A crow calls.

'Jesus fucking Christ! I drive for three and a half hours and I can't even get a hot bloody breakfast.'

Joss wanders off towards the river. She stands on the bank and listens to the small sounds of its deep determined passage.

She kicks at a pine cone. Being in the car with her father on a Sunday is not a good place to be.

'JJ! Go and help your father find some wood.' Her mother's smile is too bright as she drags the heavy picnic basket from the boot. Joss does as she is told.

'Wait for me Daddy.'

She runs after her father. He doesn't wait.

'Big or little bits Daddy? What about this bit, is it too green?'

While Joss and her mother cook bacon and eggs and make tea, her father wanders off to see if he can find a newspaper in this Godforsaken town.

Joss licks the bacon fat from her fingers. Her father turns a page of the paper. He shakes his head. 'Listen to this,' he says to her mother. He reads to her from the paper. Joss carries the plates and the billy to the river. She squats on the bank and rubs sandy mud round and round the greasy plates. She rinses off the mud with water from the billy.

They get through the morning. At twelve they go to the pub for a counter lunch. A bloke in the public bar recognizing her father from a television show he'd been in.

'Buy you a beer mate?' the bloke calls across the bar. Her father leaves Joss and her mother in the lounge.

On Monday Joss's mother makes her go to school. Joss locks her jaw and holds her feelings inside. She doesn't look at her friend. At lunchtime she goes into the chapel. She climbs the steep stairs to the choir loft where the organ is. She runs her fingers down the length of the smooth white keys and thinks about becoming a nun. The bell rings. Before Joss leaves the loft she takes one of the rosewood flutes from the box of musical instruments in the corner. If she could, she would have taken the organ.

At afternoon break her friend comes looking for her. She finds her around the side of the school, hanging off the wrought-iron gate and looking out at the park opposite.

'Hi,' she says. Joss looks at her and then looks away.

'What are you doing?'

Joss doesn't say anything. She can feel her heart in her throat and she's scared of what she'll say if she opens her mouth.

'I've got half a White Knight. You want some?'

Joss spins around.

'Why don't you go share it with Sylvie?'

'Alright I will.'

'You do then.'

'Yeah well, at least I've got friends.'

'I thought I had a friend too.'

'I didn't walk off on you. You walked off on me.'

'That's not true.'

Both girls faces are red. They are shaking and there are tears of frustration in their eyes. They scream at one another. Joss grabs hold of her friend's jumper. Her friend grabs hold of Joss's. They swing each other round until they both fall. Baring their white Cottontails to the world the two girls roll over each other across the concrete. Her friend finally pins Joss to the ground. Joss isn't angry anymore.

'You're my best friend,' she says softly.

Her friend's tears drop onto her face.

'And you're mine.'

The two girls sit up. They hold hands. Joss loves the shape of her friend's hands. They are small and soft, different to Joss's, and the nails fit neatly to the tops of the fingers, like a marble statue.

That night, Joss's father is melancholy. He pats his knee and says, 'Come here. I'll tell you a story my little mouse.'

'My story?'

'Yes, your story.

'Once upon a time, there was a lonely child locked in a cell of ice, in a warm and green country, by a witch dressed as a farmer. And there was a brave little mouse who came every day, no matter the boy's mood or silence, and patiently taught the boy to knit his dreams upon two silver knitting needles she, the little mouse, had stolen from the farmer. And when the boy could knit the air without missing a stitch and spark silver light against the ice, the mouse bought the boy a present, a ball of royal blue wool, and told the boy to knit his dreams.

'The boy did not sleep at all that night and when the mouse came the next day, the cell of ice was only walls and the boy lay on his back, looking up at a blue sky. The mouse smiled and gave the boy a ball of wool the colour of spring and went away again.

'The next day when the little mouse came the boy was rolling in spring grass. And the mouse gave the boy a ball of silver thread and told him to knit himself a mirror.

'Excited by his new-found freedom, in the smell of the wind and the touch of the grass, the boy did not question the little mouse. He simply began to knit. The mouse sat quietly on the grass and watched. When the boy was done he handed the mirror, to the mouse. But the mouse shook her head and said it was not her mirror, it was the boy's, and the boy must look into it if he wished to see himself.

'The boy was puzzled but held the mirror up and looked. And what he saw changed his life forever. For he was not a boy he was a man, a farmer, the same farmer who had locked him in the cell of ice. And behind him in the garden hidden beneath an overgrown bush of daisy was a grave, his mother's grave. And in the grave he saw his heart beating warm and strong. He had left it there as a child. And as he put his hands out to claim his heart the walls of ice melted and he was a man on a hill and it was a sunny day.'

Joss strokes her father's cheek. He takes her hand and kisses her fingertips. 'My little mouse,' he whispers.

'Come and look at this,' says her mother. She is looking out the front window. Joss climbs off her father's lap. They all look out the window.

'What?'

'There,' her mother points towards the milk bar. 'Wait.'

Suddenly orange, red and white sparks leap above Joe's fence line.

'Fireworks. It's beautiful.'

'Yeah, it is,' says her mother.

'You mean "yes" it is,' says her father. Her mother looks at him. He is smiling. Her face relaxes. It's the first open look Joss remembers between them in a long time.

'Yes. I mean "yes" it is,' she says, in an almost English accent. Joss giggles and her father almost laughs. He puts his arm around her mother and the three of them stand looking out the window watching the tiny fireworks display from Joe's backyard.

A Kind of Peace

By the end of the week life has settled back to normal. Her father rings on Friday night and says he's bringing everyone back after work.

Joss runs across to the milk bar and buys three packets of spaghetti and two lettuces. Her mother throws bacon, a little bit of cold lamb and everything else she can find into a pot to make a sauce. She will feed them all. There will even be leftovers.

Uncle Bob comes back with the rest of them. He works very hard at being one of the boys.

'Who was that woman playing the wife? She couldn't act her way out of a paper bag.'

'Well if you employ a typist as your casting lady what do you expect?' snaps her father with snake eyes.

'I couldn't agree with you more, Richard. It's not me you have to convince.'

'More wine?' One of the young boys, a would-be cameraman with sandy hair, holds the flagon of red above her father's glass.

'Always,' says her father. 'And when you've known what it's like to be so poor you drip water into the dregs of a bottle so you can at least smell wine—which you will if you stay in this business—you too will always take a glass when it is offered.'

The boy's eyes shine. He thinks her father is amazing.

That night her father passes out in the big black armchair listening to Sinatra. 'I Did it My Way,' blurs into the even scrape of the needle against the label of the record. It's still going round when Joss wakes up. She lifts the needle off and quietly goes outside with Misi.

The old man is outside Joe's, stealing a loaf of bread from the morning's delivery. Joss runs across the deserted street.

'Where have you been?' she demands, giving the old man a fright. He tries to hide the bread behind his back. Misi jumps up on him.

'Thought you went away,' he says. He bends down and scratches Misi under the chin.

'I did, but I came back.' The old man nods. He looks into Misi's eyes.

'Good girl. You're a good girl.'

'You want me to get some jam? We can have breakfast together.'

In the lane behind Joss's house, she and Misi and the old man eat bread and jam. Joss shows him the rosewood flute she stole from school. He asks her to play something. Joss closes her eyes and lets herself hear a rhythm in her head, like she does when she's alone. Joss doesn't hear notes. They come from what she's feeling. Joss plays.

The old man eases himself back and leans against the fence. He stretches his legs out across the cobbled stones and closes his eyes. Joss imagines another time when he wore a starched white shirt, the cuffs crisp against his clean washed hands.

'JJ!' Her mother calls from the back door. Joss stops playing.

'Coming Mum.' The back door slams shut. Joss stands up. The old man opens his eyes.

'See you,' she says. The old man watches her climb over the back fence. When she's inside she opens the back gate.

'Come on Misi.' The dog runs into the garden.

'Bye,' she says. 'You can keep the jam.' Joss closes the gate.

When her father had woken up, he'd gone upstairs, woken her mother and said he wanted lamb for lunch. Then he'd climbed into bed and gone back to sleep. Quietly her mother had counted out all the two and five cent pieces and now she and Joss were going shopping.

'JJ, run across to the milk bar and ask Joe if he could do with some change,' says her mother. 'There's five dollars there.'

'OK Mum.'

Joss's mother is a proud woman. She will pay the butcher in change if she has to, but she would rather not. 'Pity,' she always says to Joss, 'is something you do not want from anyone.'

'Joe says thanks. He needed change.' Joss hands her mother the five dollar note. Her mother folds it and puts it in her purse. They walk to Victoria Market. Her mother is unsure about the price of lamb. Joss feels guilty. She knows there should have been a lot more than five dollars in the change jar. That's where she takes money for the old man from.

The price of lamb is good, potatoes are cheap and mint is five cents a bunch. Joss relaxes. There's money left over. Her mother buys them both a jam donut and they catch a tram home.

Joss runs her father a bath and helps peel the potatoes.

She tries to take all the skin off each potato in one long, unbroken curly bit. She's not as good at it as her mother.

'Take these into your father,' says her mother, handing Joss two Disprin in a glass of water and the radio. 'There's a Shield match on in Sydney.'

'Oh.'

Joss puts the radio on the toilet seat and turns it on. Her father opens his eyes, she hands him the Disprin.

At twenty to one the cricketers leave the field, her father turns off the radio and gets out of the bath. Her mother carves. It is not a happy lunch. Her father does not feel like talking. As Joss clears the table there is a loud knock at the front door. Joe has finished the hull of his boat. He is taking the afternoon off. He has a bottle of grappa under his arm and a smile, as big as the sea he dreams of sailing, on his face.

'Come in. Join us, Joe,' says her father. The house is suddenly alive.

'A fiesta! We will have a fiesta. Next Saturday I will roast a whole pig. And everyone will come. The whole square.' Joe fills Joss's father's glass again. Her mother shakes her head and covers her glass with her hand.

'Salute,' says Joe.

'Salute.'

'To journeys and dreams,' says her father, grandly.

'In three years I will have her finished and then I will learn to sail.'

'Salute,' says her father.

'Salute. And then I will take my family home. But my wife she says she would rather fly.'

Everyone in the square joins in the fiesta. They drag chairs and tables into the park. Maria bakes trays of stuffed tomatoes and peppers. Timmy builds a makeshift seesaw for the kids. And the woman across the road organizes races with prizes. Joss's mother bakes scones and lamingtons and her father buys a lot of wine. Joe hangs speakers from the trees and runs the wires across the road so there will be music. He has a piano accordion and Maria's husband plays the mouth organ.

By eleven o'clock the park is transformed and everyone disappears inside to wash and dress. Joss is already dressed. She sits on the front fence kicking her legs and waiting for her friend to arrive. The smell of roasting pork makes her mouth water. Her friend is going to stay the night. Joss has never had a friend stay over before.

Her friend arrives. The girls sit on the stairs. Their mothers have coffee and chat.

'Sugar?'

'Yes, two thanks.'

'It's so good to finally meet you.'

'Yes it is. Melanie is always talking about Joss.'

'I know what you mean. They seem very close.' Both women sip. They don't ask how much the other knows about their life, their home, their secrets.

Joss and her friend win the three-legged race. They put their plates of food in a bucket Joss has tied to a long rope. They climb to the very top part of the roof at the front of Joss's house and pull the bucket up. They sit, legs straddling the carved gargoyle of the little terrace's facade, and eat their meal looking down at all the people in the park.

That night, exhausted and happy, they lie on the shaggy white rug in front of the fire and watch telly. They take it in turns to stroke the soft skin of the others forearm. It feels good. Her father comes in to get another bottle of red wine. The adults are still going in the park. Joss feels him watching them she turns her head and smiles at her father. He smiles back but his eyes are clouded. Joss thinks it's the wine. Her friend squeals and buries her head in Joss's belly.

'EXTERMINATE! EXTERMINATE!' The Daleks are coming. The girls huddle together and giggle.

Her father opens the wine slowly. Joss can feel him watching them on the carpet. Their legs tangle, intimate. Joss's friend is getting breasts. Her long hair is dark against the white rug. Joss laughs and stretches out beside her.

Her mother comes through from the kitchen carrying a basket of rolls. She stops in the hallway and looks at Joss's father. He turns away and pulls the cork.

Joss and her friend sleep well together. Top-to-tail and back-to-back. Their bottoms fit into the curve of the other's legs.

Her friend's mother comes early next morning, ten-thirty. The girls beg and plead to be able to stay together longer. Their mothers smile indulgently but they have things to do. Joss waves her friend goodbye.

When she comes inside her mother has started cleaning out the fireplace, her father is still asleep and the house feels empty. Joss doesn't know what to do. She goes upstairs and lies on her bed. She can feel her organs shifting inside, her heart and her lungs and her stomach, whispering feelings she doesn't understand.

Joss's father is in a bad mood when he gets up.

'Do you want a cup of tea darling?' asks her mother.

'No. I want a fucking drink.' Joss closes her bedroom door. She takes out her ink and drawing book and sits on the floor.

When her mother calls her downstairs for lunch Joss tries to leave her shifting feelings pressed between the drawings in her book. Girls, dancing in a forest. Horses, manes and tails blowing in the wind. Joss usually draws trees.

She and her mother eat at the dining-room table. Her father eats in front of the telly. Her mother is tense and trying not to show it. Joss dunks bread into her soup.

Her father walks through from the lounge room. He is drunk. He leans against the wall and looks at them.

'Chatty, aren't you?' He's dripped soup down the front of his shirt. Joss looks away. The black dog is stirring.

'Do you want some more soup, I'll get it for you.' Her mother pushes back her chair to stand.

'No, I don't want any more fucking soup, thank you.' Unsteadily he heads for the bathroom. Joss and her mother listen. The weight of alcohol is in the long slow stream of piss against the porcelain. He doesn't flush. A bathroom cupboard slams. Joss puts down her spoon.

When he comes back he has a pair of scissors in his hand.

'Come here,' he says to Joss. 'Your hair's too long.'

Joss looks at her mother. Her mother reaches across the table for the bowls but does not look at her.

'Hang on,' her mother says. 'While I get you a towel.'

Joss sits between her father's legs and he cuts her hair, short, like a boy's.

The next morning before school her mother takes Joss to the hairdressers.

'Can you soften it?' she says to the lady with long bright nails behind the counter. 'We'd like something, gamine. Sort of French.'

That night her father comes and tucks her in. He traces the lines of her small, chiselled face. He smells sweet, like brandy, but his eyes are clear.

'You know, if it wasn't for me you wouldn't be here.'

'What do you mean?'

'Your mother never wanted children. But I did. Lots and lots of children. At least I've got you, eh?'

Her mother makes porridge for breakfast the next morning. Joss watches the butter melt into yellow rivers running through white mountains.

'Eat up, honey, you'll be late for school,' says her mother. There are bruises on her arms. Her father calls from the bedroom.

'Where are my bloody socks?'

'In the second drawer.' Her mother runs up the stairs. Joss gives her porridge to the dog.

The Company

Joss turns ten, double figures, a few weeks before the end of school, in late November. She is given a new box of paints and her mother has a little party for her after school, before her father comes home. Joss doesn't know who to invite so she invites three girls her friend likes. She even invites Sylvie Gorgon. When the girls go home Joss cuts a big slice of birthday cake, puts some port in an old soda water bottle and goes to look for the old man. He lights a match and sings her 'Happy Birthday'.

Her father is in a good mood when he comes home. He swings her mother round and slaps her on the bum. He pokes at Joss and riles her up.

'You want to play do you? You want to wrestle eh? Come on Midget you better get your referee's whistle out.'

Midget. Her father hasn't called her mother that for ages. Her mother comes through from the kitchen, wiping her hands on a blue-and-white check tea towel. She pushes the hair back off her face with the back of her hand. She is smiling but uncertain. When her father is in a good mood, Joss and her mother don't have a choice; they are too. But his good moods are always unsettling. You never know where they'll lead.

'Ding a ling a ling,' calls her mother. Joss and her father come out of their corners. Her father throws Joss onto her back. She's fast. She's up. Spinning around, she attacks from behind. Misi joins the skirmish. Hands and legs and tails and teeth.

'Ding a ling a ling! Back to your corners.'

Joss and her father retreat. They both lean forward, hands on their knees, catching their breath, eyeing each other with the will of adversaries.

The outcome is always the same, in the fourth round, her father lets her win. He pins her to the ground, she feels his strength, then he lets her slide from under him and flatten him by sitting on his back. He groans and moans while she counts to three and is declared the winner.

Her father stands and brushes himself off. 'OK. Go and make your mother and I a drink. And then we're going out for dinner.' Joss sees the tension stretch across her mother's face. She drops her voice. 'Richard we can't. We can't afford it.'

He laughs. He's playing with her.

'You mean you won't take your family out to dinner?'

'Of course I would. But . . .'

'I'd have thought now you were a working woman?' He turns and struts across the tiny lounge room. Her mother's face has gone white. The sandwich bar, he's found out. Her mother shoots Joss a look. Joss eyes say, 'I didn't tell him Mummy. I didn't.'

'How are those drinks coming along?' calls her father.

'Nearly done, Daddy.'

Her mother reels in all her feelings and laughs lightly. 'Richard, I don't know what you're talking about.'

He turns.

'You . . . are the new casting lady of Australian Drama.'

'What? I don't understand.'

'It's simple. We needed a new casting lady. I suggested you. They thought it was a great idea.'

'But Richard?'

'Don't be ridiculous. You know actors and you know the business. And I am sick to death of having to deal with some accountant secretary who thinks a 'cameo' is a kind of brooch!'

Her mother stands in the middle of the room with her mouth open.

'Well, what's wrong with you?' demands her father.

'I. I guess I just would have liked to have been asked.'

'Oh for Christ sake. Don't be so Goddamn precious.' And with that Joss's mother starts a new full-time job and Joss starts going to Maria's after school.

Maria feeds Joss Teddy Bear biscuits and sweet milk coffee. She tells her she must always be a good girl not like her daughter, 'who wears her skirts too short and takes her shoes off like a Gypsy.' Maria says these things very loudly so her daughter will hear her. Maria's daughter hardly ever comes out of her bedroom.

Her bedroom is tiny, posters of pop stars plastered between the gold-framed paintings of the Virgin Mary and Christ on Calvary.

No matter how hard Joss tries Maria's daughter will not talk to her.

At lunchtime about a week before the end of school, Ann with the ringlets and sand-flat voice throws all her clothes out the classroom window.

Joss and her friend barge into the grade three classroom to get some paper to make paper aeroplanes and freeze. Ann is standing by the window. A fat girl from grade four, whose name Joss can never remember, is standing in front of Ann.

'Go on,' says the fat girl. 'I dare you.'

Ann takes her underpants off.

'Big deal,' says the fat girl. About ten little girls in neat sailor uniforms stand around watching, not saying a word. Everyone's frightened of the fat girl. They all know what you've got to do to be in her gang. You've got to stick a piece of licorice up yourself while she watches and then eat it. Joss doesn't understand why she wants people to do that.

'You're a fucker,' spits Ann as she rips her uniform off and throws it out the window.

'Yeah well, you can talk,' says the fat girl and she puts her hand between Ann's legs. Joss and her friend run out of the classroom. They hide behind the chapel and don't know how to look at each other.

At night, in between the dreams of hit and fear, Joss finds the strengths she will need for the next day. Somewhere in her dreaming she collects a feather, a stone, a grain of sand and places them in a leather pouch she dreams she wears around her waist.

'JJ! JJ, it's eight-thirty. You've got mass this morning. And I'm late.' Half-conscious Joss climbs from her dreams. Her mother's standing beside her bed, already dressed and made-up.

'You like your job, don't you Mum.'

'Yes. Yes I do.' Her mother holds up her school uniform.

'Come on.'

The schoolyard is deserted. Joss runs down the covered walkway leading to the chapel. Her footsteps echo in the playground. A single note from the organ and the choir begins to sing.

'Sing, sing a song of joy for men shall love each other.'

Joss opens the chapel door and slips inside. Sister Beatrice's eyes lock onto her like a hawk.

'That day will come just as sure as hearts that are pure are hearts set free.'

Joss genuflects and slides into the grade three pew.

'You're late,' says her friend.

'I know.'

'Sing, sing a song of joy for men shall love each other.'

Joss looks along the two rows of grade three girls. She is looking for Ann.

'She's not here,' whispers her friend.

'Oh.'

Ann doesn't come back to school. No-one mentions what happened. Sister Beatrice doesn't even call her name out on the roll.

The Wardrobe Mistress

It is the first Monday of the holidays and Joss's mother is in a flap. She's on the phone trying to find someone to look after Joss. Maria's mother's died, her husband's sick; something's happened.

Maria came to their house at eight o'clock, knocked lightly on the front door and whispered in Joss's mother's ear. Ever since then her mother has been on the phone. In a flap and on the phone. Joss said she'd stay home by herself. Her mother told her not to be stupid. So Joss left her to it. She went up to her room to lie on her bed with Misi and wait.

Joss hears her mother on the stairs. She sits up. Her mother comes and stands in the doorway.

'There's nothing for it. You'll have to come with me.'

'It's alright Mum. I'll be good.'

Joss has been to her father's work before but only on Friday nights when she and her mother were invited to join her father and the family in the boardroom for drinks. Uncle Rupert, Uncle Bob, Uncle John, Uncle Josh, Aunty Irene and Aunty Sarah.

'Come in! Come in,' Uncle Rupert would say. 'Clair it's so good to see you. What would you like to drink?' And then he would turn his attention to Joss. 'What a big girl you're becoming. Come and give your Uncle Rupert a kiss.' And then he would get Joss a glass of lemonade and she would sit quietly on a green leather chair at the boardroom table and swing her legs, while everyone laughed and talked and thumped the table to emphasize their point. But Joss had never been free to explore the dusty nooks and crannies of the sprawling city building where both her parents now worked.

Joss and her mother step out of a taxi into the morning bustle of Collins Street. Her father has been at work since seven. Her mother holds Joss by the wrist. Joss withholds her arm slightly, a gesture that says,'Mum I'm ten.' Her mother ignores it. They cross the road and walk toward the old building of stone and carved granite. The peaks of the roof are decorated with filigree and gargoyles. They walk up three steps, through wrought-iron gates that open into a wide hallway of pale green, polished linoleum. Decades of dust banished to the corners. Tiny offices honeycomb off the main hallway; solicitors, surveyors, accountants. Her mother's work is upstairs, her father's work is next door.

There is a lift but her mother never uses it. When you press the button you hear a clunk and whirr. It's a shaky old thing. The stairs are wide with a solid wooden banister and windows that look out onto the grey wall of the building next door.

As soon as her mother steps into her office, she's busy.

'The contract I drew up for Stewart's been rejected by his agent,' says her mother's secretary. 'Oh Hi, JJ. What should I do about it?' Joss backs out of the office.

'JJ!'

Joss pokes her head back in.

'Where are you going?'

'I'm just going to have a look around.' The phone rings.

'Well don't get in anyone's way, alright.'

'I won't.'

It's the back of the building that's most interesting to Joss. There are tiny padded sound-booths that look like Dr Who's Tardis and storage cages for all the props. It's a wonderland of bits and pieces. A metal security door opens into the upstairs of the building next door and Joss finds herself in a room filled with feathers, gowns and sequins, two desks, a red-haired woman and a blond-haired man in tight pants. The front wall of the room is a window that looks down onto the rehearsal room where her father is.

'And what have we here? It's a piccaninny. My God it's a piccaninny,' says the blond man.

'This is Jocelyn, Richard and Clair's daughter,' says the red-haired woman.

A high pitched 'Oh' escapes the blond man's lips.

'You don't remember me, do you?'

Joss wonders if she should lie. She doesn't. She shakes her head.

'My name's Dot. I knew you when you were a little girl. Are you on holidays?' Joss nods. 'Do you feel like doing some work? Mark and I could do with an extra pair of hands.'

'OK.'

Joss spends the next three weeks of her holidays in the wardrobe department. Dot and Mark don't treat her like a child. Mark talks about his boyfriend and Dot makes rude jokes about actors' penises not being the size of their egos. Sometimes Joss helps, fetching doubles of the clothes they have chosen for different actors. But most of the time she plays in the back rooms surrounded by costumes. She dresses up in feathers and hoops and lacy bodices. Big wooden windows open onto the lead roof of the building next door and let light into the back rooms of the wardrobe department. Hundreds of pigeons roost there. Joss can walk out onto the roof and if she takes food the birds don't fly away. There are nests in the cracked air vents of the wall and fat birds sit on pale speckled eggs. Joss likes the pigeons. She pretends she's the bird woman from *Mary Poppins*. She sings, and scatters doughnut crumbs across the lead roof, losing herself in the flapping of wings.

'You're not a singer, I'm afraid Darling,' says Mark, his head sticking out the window. 'But then I'm not a Wardrobe Mistress. Still, we can but dream.' Joss laughs. Mark always makes her laugh. He climbs out onto the roof and hands her half a jam donut.

After Dot and Mark leave at night Joss sits on Dot's desk and looks down on her father in the rehearsal room.

All the sets are marked out on the floor with different coloured masking tape. There are a couple of old tables and chairs, an old bed base and a kind of bench, which her father and Uncle John slide in and out of the marked spaces. Her father is wonderful to watch down there on the floor with the actors. He uses his hands when he talks. He plays all their roles and shows them how to move. Joss thinks about how you notice him above everyone else in the room.

Her father leads people. Like the Pied Piper, they follow him down Collins Street and into the Federal Hotel, into the Grand Dining Room. It's Friday night. He orders drinks; whisky, gin, wine and scotch and a lemonade for Joss. Everyone leans across the table talking. The actors all try and out-actor each other. Joss hopes they order soon. She's hungry.

'We'll never get this new show off the ground.'

'Never say never. You're talking to the boy who taught himself to read by candlelight,' says her father.

It's late. Joss is on her second dessert. She can see the reflection of the dining room's crystal chandelier in the caramel glaze on her custard. Her mother has her back to her and is talking to a young actress who is working for her father this week. This is the young actress's first television job and she keeps telling Joss's mother how grateful she is for the opportunity.

'Hey Richard!' Barry calls across the table at her father. 'Did you hear about the fucking cops at La Mama?'

Joss puts a spoonful of custard in her mouth and looks at her father. La Mama is the little theatre up the road from their house.

'Yeah, I heard.'

'Well what do you think?'

'I think the majority of the actors who perform at La Mama would do a lot better to learn their craft before trying to make political statements.'

'Come on. Don't tell me you agree with all this censorship shit.'

'I think there's more to writing a good play than obscenities.'

'Have you seen the play? I have. It's bloody good.'

Her father stands and leans across the table. Everyone stops talking. 'You would be nothing without the words I put in your mouth. You don't even know how to read a Goddamn television script. What would you know about a good play?' Her father has put a rapier right through Barry's heart. There's an awful silence at the table.

Joss's mother's face is red.

'Hey come on, Richard,' says Uncle John putting his hand on her father's arm. Her father laughs, smiles at Barry like a mate.

'Don't look so shit-scared. You're young. You're a star.

I'm a crotchety old bastard who told Otto Preminger to get fucked. Only actor who ever did, so I'm told.'

Everyone laughs. The tension breaks and slowly people begin to talk again.

That night the black dog stalks the dolls' house.

'Embarrass you last night, did I?' her father asks her mother over breakfast. Joss's mother doesn't know what to say. Joss is in the kitchen making toast. She watches her mother search for safe words. If she says no, he'll accuse her of lying and he'll be right. If she says yes, he'll get angry. Joss slams the knife and fork drawer shut, jamming her fingers. She doesn't think to do it. She just does it.

'Ow Daddy,' she cries, it does hurt.

'Jesus!' says her father standing up from the dining-room table. He comes into the kitchen. When he sees the tears in Joss's eyes and her hand jammed in the drawer he changes.

'Little mouse,' he says. 'How did you do that?'

He pulls the drawer open and picks her up. She buries her head into his shoulder. He carries her through to the lounge room, sits down in the big black chair and puts her on his knee. He kisses her fingers. Her mother comes in with iceblocks wrapped in a tea towel. She kneels down and wraps the ice around Joss's fingers.

'Just remember who got you your job,' her father says to her mother and then he tells her to turn on the telly.

The rest of the weekend passes without incident. They even get through Sunday. Joss finds the old man and tells him about the pigeons. He has a headache. Joss gets him Disprin from their bathroom cupboard but he says he ain't goin' to take no drugs. 'No thank you.' So Joss takes them. She likes the taste of Disprin.

On Monday morning when Joss bounces into the wardrobe department, Dot is in a fluster.

'Jocelyn can you iron?'

'I think so.'

'Thank God. Of all days for Mark to take off sick.' Dot lays fifteen pink-sequined dresses out on a table beside the ironing-board.

'I don't know if I can iron those,' says Joss.

'No darling, you don't have to iron them. Just the hems. They're an inch too long. We're going to take them up.'

Joss's mother never lets Joss use the iron on her own. She's always scared Joss'll burn herself. But Joss doesn't burn herself once doing the pink dresses. It's not hard. It makes her wonder why her mother's so frightened of the iron.

After they finish, Dot sends Joss downstairs to buy two milkshakes and a sticky bun. Dot is English and, compared to the people she works with, she is very quiet and restrained. She dresses beautifully and always paints her nails the palest shade of apricot.

Joss licks the coffee icing off her fingers. Dot pushes Joss's hair back off her face. She tries to fluff it with her long fingers but it falls back, flat.

'I think you should grow your hair a little,' she says. 'You're growing up. You don't need it to be so short anymore.'

Joss suddenly feels messy and awkward.

'I'm not very good at doing hair,' she says.

'You'll learn,' says Dot, reaching across the table for the pink hemming thread.

Her father had said that to her once when she was six.

She was in the garden, dancing. Yellow chiffon flowing behind her, twisting around her. Pretty.

Suddenly her father lifted her by one arm. Her feet

walked the air. His face was over hers, his mouth spitting. The garden vanished. The stairs hit hard on her hip, the bedroom door hard against her back. He ripped the dress off.

'You disgusting little bitch . . . '

There were gashes across Joss's memory.

'You malicious little bitch . . . ' He took the belt from his pants. His words went on and on.

Joss stood in the middle of the room, in her white Cottontails, tears running down her face. 'Where's Mummy,' she whispered and he hit out with his belt, the buckled end. It struck Joss behind the knee knocking her to the ground. Her mother didn't come.

He lifted her with one arm and carried her to the bed and laying her across his knee, ripped the pants from her bottom. Pulling the crotch hard between her legs.

He hit and hit and then he threw her on the bed. But before he slammed the bedroom door shut he said, 'You'll learn.'

And she did.

She learnt to listen for small sounds and think of herself as a boy. It was safer.

At Christmas drinks in the boardroom, when Uncle Rupert asks Joss what she wants for Christmas, she says a bowie knife. Everyone laughs. Out of the corner of her eye, Joss sees her father's satisfied smile before he sips his drink. The tight place inside dissolves.

The River

Her mother finishes work a week before Christmas. Joss misses going to the office.

The night her father finishes work he comes home with holiday pay. He drags them out to do the town. He drinks a lot and orders oysters for them all. Smiling, Joss holds her breath and swallows. She eats a dozen oysters in a minute and a half. Her father is pleased. He orders her two desserts and starts to sing.

'Che gelida manina.'

My tiny hand is frozen.

Her father takes her hand across the table.

'Se la lasci riscaldar.'

He draws her towards him. She is part of the show.

'Cercar che giova.'

She sits on his knee. She looks up at him. Her father's not a very good singer. She would like to look at the people at the other tables.

'Al buio non si trovo.'

Suddenly the double doors leading from the kitchen of the Italian bistro swing open and their waiter, in a crisp white shirt with a black cummerbund and a white linen cloth draped over his right forearm, begins to sing.

'Ma per fortuno è una notte di luna, e qui la luna e'abbiamo vicina.'

His voice is like the ocean picking up her father's voice and carrying it. Unleashing a sea amongst the marinara and the wine goblets.

Her father wakes up in the morning with a hangover. He says her mother let him drink too much. He has a raw egg in tomato juice with a dash of Worcestershire sauce and goes outside to pack the car.

They are going away. Back to a place Joss never remembers having been. 'That's because you hadn't been born yet,' says her mother, yanking up the leather straps on the old wicker picnic basket and fastening the buckles.

Outside, her father is strapping tent poles to the roof-rack with a hairy rope—the one they'll put around the tent to keep the snakes out. He smiles at her across the roof of the car and his eyes wrinkle. 'I'm taking you to the Big River,' he says. He steps off the running board, his head disappears behind the bulk of their tent already tied tight. Joss can see his body through the car windows.

Joss's first glimpse of the river is early in the morning. They have driven for two days. This is the third and they have been driving since four in the morning. It is ten to nine and the sun is warming. For the last half an hour they have been driving away from the main highway, and the other cars filled with holiday-makers, through rich, wet farmland where corn and sugarcane grow. Suddenly the narrow black road turns and runs down into the river. Her father stops the car at a white boom gate and opens his door. Misi jumps out first, before her father's foot can even touch the ground, and disappears into the tall grass. Her father stretches. Joss gets out of the car.

No-one speaks. The quiet is alive. Her father walks out onto the small pier. Her mother follows. Joss looks across the river. Mist rises off the water. She can't see the opposite bank. She ducks under the boom gate and walks down the road into the water. It's cool on her feet. By the time she's knee deep, she can feel the whispers of a cold current. Thick steel cables run up out of the water and are pegged in the bitumen with giant's nails, rusted and pitted with age.

Joss hears the ferry before she sees it. The river sends the sound to them all the way from the other side. A few minutes later the ferry emerges out of the mist. The crossing takes about fifteen minutes. By the time the ferry has docked, other cars are waiting to cross and the mist is clearing. The sun is hot on Joss's back now; dry hot.

Joss loops a rope through Misi's collar and walks her onto the ferry. Her father chats to a man in a ute who has parked beside him. They lean against the bonnets of their cars. Joss hears her father say 'mate' and 'how's the fishing been?' before the engines of the ferry start up with a clang and an even Chuga-chuga-chuga-chuga, Chuga-chuga-chuga-chuga, that pushes them out into the river.

Joss leans out over the railings and looks down. The water pushes one way and the ferry cuts across it, the thick steel cables straining.

The old ferryman comes and stands beside her. He wipes his hands on an oily rag. Between the smudges of oil and grease are tiny yellow rosebuds, the kind you get on sheets. The old ferryman eyes the river.

'It's a big river,' says Joss.

'It's a fuckin' dangerous river,' says the ferryman, not taking his eyes from the straining cables. 'Rivers are meant to flow to the sea. Not this one. She pushes up like a stranger trying to belong. Don't you go swimmin' in her now. Sharks come up for breeding.'

Joss looks at the dark water. She hates sharks. Even at ten, she still sits on the plug in the bath and keeps one eye on the tap, just in case.

Her father calls Joss. They're going to drive off the ferry. Everyone revs their cars as the ferry docks. The air smells.

Four miles down a narrow road, that winds along the banks of the river, is a handpainted sign saying Lawrence, population 46. There is a general store, of unpainted weatherboards with a wide verandah and a Peters Ice cream sign, on the right. Opposite, on the bank of the river, is a playground; a rusted swing and a slide and a wizzy-dizzy, overgrown with grass. Around the bend is a pretty weatherboard house, a little further up a not so pretty one and then a pub. Her father pulls their car in under one of the huge Moreton Bay fig trees on the banks of the river. He disappears across the road to the pub. Joss gets out and climbs the tree. The branches are smooth. It's a friendly tree to climb, green, water-rich leaves. Her father strides back across the road.

'No problem!' He begins to unpack. Joss's mother is quick to help. Joss slides down out of the tree.

'What can I do Daddy?' Her father is struggling with their huge canvas tent.

'Keep out of the bloody way.'

Joss heads off up the river, to explore. Outside the township the river turns inland, cutting its way through fields of tall grass. Joss is caught by the shifting patterns. She watches. The grass bends one way. Then another. She is watching the wind. Watching the swollen heads of grass bend to its will. Sensations that she doesn't have words for rise and fade into the day with the passing of a breeze, as though they had never been. Joss is gone for hours.

When she wanders back, the tent is up. Her mother is making it into a home and her father is fishing on the river, in a small red rowboat. Joss starts collecting wood. She and her mother make a fire.

Joss sees her father reel in his line and begin to row for the shore. She squats in the grass and watches him battle the current that wants to take him upstream—the tide has changed since the morning. She tugs out a piece of grass, puts the thick end of the stem in her mouth. Her father isn't getting anywhere. He's rowing on the spot. She bites into the grass. It's summer sweet. She nibbles at it. Her father breaks the lock of the current and begins to move. It takes him a long time to reach the shore.

After dinner, with fingers sticky from fish, Joss and her mother decorate a small gum near their tent. Her father's not one for Christmas. He goes to the pub. Joss watches him stride through the long grass and across the road. An old Holden pulls up outside the pub. Six children tumble out, squabbling and laughing. Her father steps onto the verandah, walks around the side and disappears into the public bar. It's dusk. Watercolour red and yellow spread across the sky. Her father calls dusk the little death.

Her mother nimbly threads a piece of grass though the metal loop on the top of a Christmas decoration she bought twenty-three years ago in England. Joss picks up a little red house with snow on the roof and sticks it in a fork of the tree. She doesn't care much for Christmas either. She tries to imagine being in England: green hills, leafy oak trees, Robin Hood and snow. There, Christmas must mean something. But her imagining is only pictures; all her senses are in her bare feet on the ground, where she can feel the thrumming of the earth. Her feet are soft with dust and already her soles are hardening.

It is dark when Joss and her mother finish decorating the tree. Her mother finds a torch and they walk to the pub. Women and children sit on the verandah, enjoying the cool, eating chips and drinking lemonade. Her mother pokes her head into the public bar. The men stop talking. Her father turns around. 'A drink?' he asks. Her mother nods and goes to find them a table on the verandah. Joss hangs over the balcony watching the kids play chasey in the car park.

'Here JJ!' calls her mother. Joss goes and sits next to her. The window into the bar is open. Two men are arguing about some new-fangled tractor. Joss kneels up and looks in. Her father has bought her a raspberry lemonade. He hands the barmen a five dollar note and waits for his change. Suddenly the old man sitting at the end of the bar slams his fist down and stands up.

'Fuck me dead! It's either Richard Clarkson or Clark Richardson!'

Her father stares at the old bloke. 'Ken?'

'Too bloody right! You old bastard! What are you doing here? Where's the Mrs?'

'Outside.'

'Jesus.'

Ken and her father carry the drinks out. When Ken sees her mother, he looks like he is going to cry. He wraps her mother in his farmers arms and pats her on the back. He is a big man used to dealing with cows.

'And Stella?' asks Joss's mother holding his face in her hands.

'She's right bloody here. Hey Mother!'

Out of the shadows on the verandah Stella appears. A woman in a light cotton shift, with arms soft like butter pastry. Joss's father stands.

'Oh my Lord!' pants Stella. She braces herself against the railing. 'It is,' she pants.

'You beautiful woman,' says her father, moving towards Stella. He hugs her with respect, holding in his own strength. Stella laughs like a young girl.

Stella is the happiest person Joss has ever met. She has a hole in her heart. She is dying.

'But it's not as big as it used to be,' says Ken authoritatively. He looks at Joss and motions his head in the direction of her mother and father. 'Thanks to these two buggers. You come from good stock, honey.'

'Cut it out, Ken,' Joss's father is embarrassed. Joss has never seen him like that before. Stella laughs. Her breath whistles through the hole in her heart.

'It was them who got me to that city hospital, nearly sixteen years ago now.'

'Stella!' says her father shifting his weight like a boy.

'A fact's a fact. Got the doctors to put a ticker thing in. The silly old bugger at Grafton told me I only had six months. And I'm still here.' She laughs. 'Tickles me fancy that.'

'Alright, alright. Want another drink?' Joss's father has blushed.

Stories tumble out of her father's mouth. When he tells the Otto Preminger story, it's different. There are cracks where he seeps out.

'Otto who?' asks Ken.

'*Exodus* mate. You remember that film.'

'Too right I do. Who was he in it?'

'He directed it.'

'Bloody hell. What do you know.'

Laughter. Ken shakes his head.

'Always wondered what them directors really do.'

'What do you do when it's time for that prize sow of yours to mate?'

'I hire a good stud, stick him in a pen with her and watch.'

'That's what a director does. He just has a camera.'

Everyone cracks up. Her father has sent himself up.

He goes on and tells them about her mother nearly losing the baby on the trip back from England. How she wasn't allowed out of bed and all she wanted was oysters.

'Seemed bloody ridiculous. I mean there we were bobbing up and down on the Goddamn ocean and there weren't any bloody oysters.'

He tells them how he scoured Bombay trying to buy some for her mother when the ship docked there for a day. How in India it's easier to buy pearls. How when he finally did find some, the fisherman made him pay through the nose and how, on the way back to the ship, he ate three of them because he wasn't quite sure they were fresh. He tells Stella and Ken he fully expected to die.

'It's the writer in me,' he says. *Death on an Indian Dock!* They laugh.

'When you didn't die, what'd you do?' gasps Stella. Laughing takes it out of her.

'I cooked them up in the galley myself, with Worcestershire sauce and bacon and served them to my lady on a silver plate.'

'You probably bloody did too,' says Ken shaking his head.

'He did,' says her mother. 'And they were the best I've ever eaten.'

Her father puts his hand on the back of Joss's neck and gives a little squeeze.

'Good thing you never told her what colour they were,' says Ken.

'Why do you think I cooked them.'

A gust of laughter sweeps over the table. Joss has never seen her father like this with people before. She is old enough to think it strange he should be like this with a farmer and his wife, who say 'come' instead of 'came' and don't know who Otto Preminger is.

Her father is different with Stella and Ken, on the river and around the camp fire. Joss decides walls are the problem. When they lived in a tent her parents didn't fight.

'Well the bloody flood of '56 nearly did us in,' says Ken. 'If mother hadn't taught six of our best to swim we'd have been rooted. There she was, swimin' round. Her dress floatin' up under her arms. Puffin' and pantin' and beatin' those bloody cows on the backside with a bloody broom.'

Everyone laughs.

'More frightened of mother than the flood, they were.'

Joss gets up and goes to the edge of the verandah. Kids race across the dusty car park, skidding in and out of shadows and sliding under cars. She hangs over the railing and watches them.

Three little ones shove and push and talk in loud whispers. They are planning an ambush. A tall boy comes racing round the side of the pub. They nab him. One grabs his ankles, the other leaps on his back and the third is so excited he just jumps up and down laughing and screeching.

'You're it! You're it!'

The tall boy rolls around in the dust with them, growling and snarling. When he stands up they scatter like wild ducks. He squats in the shadows, closes his eyes and counts to ten.

'Comin' ready or not!'

His eyes meet Joss's across the car park. Joss does a spin over the balcony railing. She is strong. The boy notices. He puts on a good show of looking for the little ones. He gets close but doesn't spring them. He nabs an older kid, hiding in a tree.

'Wanna play?' says one of the little kids looking up at Joss. She looks at the tall boy. 'Well, do you?' he says.

Joss swings down off the balcony. 'Yeh, OK.' They don't tell each other their names.

They play until the pub closes and their parents wander down into the dusty car park with blurred grins on their faces. Children attach themselves to parents, and the ragtail clusters disappear into the warm darkness until all that is left is the sound of laughter coming from somewhere down the road.

Christmas

On Christmas morning, Joss wakes up to find a grey and white plastic cat, in a pillowcase, at the foot of her bed. The cat is filled with sticky toffees, each one wrapped in stripy tinsel paper. Two days before Joss had seen the cat at the general store, on a shelf between the potatoes and fishing tackle.

Joss pulls out the plastic stopper under the cat's bottom and takes out a toffee. Her parents are sleeping. She pops the toffee into her mouth and pulls on a pair of shorts and a T-shirt. She tiptoes out of the tent. A twig snaps under the groundsheet.

The toffee gets stuck in Joss's teeth. She pushes it with her tongue and sucks at it. Her sucking fills her ears with such a big sound she fears it will wake her parents. Joss stops sucking and listens. There is no other noise. Only she and the sun are awake. Joss has never noticed how noisy eating is before. She spits out the toffee. She crosses the road, climbs the fence behind the pub and walks into the bush.

The dust of the earth is cool. Dry grasses whisper, Joss walks soft-footed, drawn into the morning.

A blackbird flies screaming from a ghost gum. Joss feels the sun's rays hot on her back. She's been gone a long time. Her parents will be up. She turns and runs back towards the pub, the bush brittle under her bare feet, the dreaming gone. By the time she reaches the fence behind the pub she is sweating. She quickly gathers wood and hurries back to the tent.

Her mother is dressing. Her father is lighting the fire. Joss's stomach is tight. She dumps her armload of wood.

'Morning Daddy,' she gives her father a big kiss.

'Morning little mouse.' He hands her the billy. 'Fill this will you.' The knot in her stomach loosens. Joss goes and fills the billy.

Her mother cooks kippers for breakfast. They're her father's favourite. After breakfast and the ABC radio news her father hands Joss a small package.

'Happy Christmas.' His smile is lopsided.

Joss unwraps the package, it's a knife, for gutting fish, it is as close to a bowie knife as he could find.

After breakfast Joss washes in a bucket on the edge of the river. She won't go swimming no matter how much her mother coaxes. Finally her mother turns, 'Suit yourself,' she says and pushes out into the water. Joss's father is standing on a sandbank in the middle of the river, his bathers dripping and his hat still on. Her mother moves through the current towards him. Her mother swims like a lady, she never gets her hair wet and only does sidestroke.

Joss tips a bucket of water over her head and lathers up with Velvet soap, they are going to Stella and Ken's for Christmas lunch.

'Mischief!' Her father's voice booms across the water. Joss opens one eye against the soap. Misi leaps off the bank. Joss grabs for her. But the dog is quick.

'Here girl! Come on,' calls her father. Misi's little legs work fast against the current. Joss can feel her heart in her chest. Soap runs into her eye, she rubs at it and opens the other one. Any minute, any minute a shark will come. Joss can see it, a dark shadow coming up under her dog's little legs. At the last minute there will be teeth.

Misi stumbles on the edge of the sandbank and trots out of the water shaking herself. Joss's father pats Joss's dog.

Misi runs up and down the sandbank, barking. Joss's father puts his arm around Joss's mother and points at something down the river. Joss can feel her heart, angry. She scoops a bucket of water from the river and tips it over her head.

The track into Stella and Ken's is corrugated, hard, red soil. There are three gates. Joss is the gate girl. The farmhouse is on stilts, Joss sees it from the second gate. It is weatherboard and unpainted. Inside Ken shows them the floodmarks on the walls. The house is simple and smells of milk and tobacco. There is a big boot room at the back, with a bench where Ken skins rabbits. He gives Joss a rabbit's tail for good luck. It is soft and white, she rubs it across her cheek.

They eat wild pig for lunch, with apple sauce and potato salad. For dessert, Stella has picked blackberries, she puts dollops of cold, fresh cream on top. After lunch everyone stretches out under the ceiling fan. Stella and her mother talk.

'Whatever happened to that nice Sister? The one that was a friend of yours,' pants Stella.

'Oh, she's still in Sydney, nursing. Now we're in Melbourne I don't see her much.'

'Been meaning to write to her for years.'

Ken and her father talk.

'The bastard floored him! He's a bloody brilliant bowler.'

'I don't know about that,' says Ken shaking his head slowly. 'If the pitch is hard and dry, you might just find that English bowler of yours comes a cropper.'

Joss goes outside.

She walks down the track that leads past the milking shed. Stella calls from the back steps.

'There's quicksand over there in the marshes!' She points and holds the doorframe to catch her breath. Ken comes up behind her and calls over her shoulder, finishing what she had wanted to say, 'Best not to go there love!'

Joss waves. They go back inside.

Joss climbs the fence leading down to the creek. She stops and fills her pockets with stones and then curves back towards the marshes. She's never seen quicksand. Her gumboots make her heavy-footed. She takes them off and leaves them by a stump. She's not scared of snakes, she knows how to make a vaccine.

The track is narrow and damp, winding through tall marsh grasses. Joss squeezes the earth between her toes as she walks. Across a fallen log there is a flat patch of luminous green, creeping grass. It's different; maybe it's quicksand. Joss squats and throws a stone into the middle of it. Nothing happens. She throws a handful. Nothing. She walks on.

Steam rises from the damp earth and dries on Joss's thighs. The distance shimmers with heat. Joss is alone in the world. The bush does that to her. Whispers turn to voices, her blood thins and quickens. She is looking for quicksand and the trees are singing.

That night, leaning back in his deckchair by the camp fire, looking up at the black star night, a drink in his hand, her father seems happy. 'Wonder what the rich people are doing?' he says.

The next four days fade one into another. Her father fishing on the river, her mother by his side, baiting hooks and threading tackle. In the late afternoon he listens to the cricket, while her mother cooks. When it's dark they go to the pub. All Joss has to do is collect wood and gut the fish, the rest of the time is hers. She spends it in the bush. She meets the boy from the pub, the tall one. He shows her a cave. His father shoots roos. He never tells her his name but he shows her his penis.

On the fifth day there is a funeral. The graveyard is on top of the hill behind the general store. A dusty red truck turns and bumps up the dirt road with a coffin on the back. Joss watches from the corner. There are a few old cars filled with women and children but no men, until out of the bush come twenty horsemen dressed in black.

After the funeral the women and children get back into their cars and follow the red truck out of town. The men, on their horses, follow the truck as far as the pub. Joss runs along the river bank following the horsemen. She stops at the corner of their tent, opposite the pub, and watches the men tether their horses and silently disappear into the public bar.

Out on the river Joss sees her mother and father rowing in. She hurries into the tent and washes for dinner. She puts on clean shorts. Tonight her father is going to recite Banjo Paterson at the pub. The publican had asked him and invited them for a counter tea at six.

The atmosphere in the pub is tense. Joss and her mother and father are the only ones in the ladies' lounge. They order three T-bone steaks and her father asks the publican what's going on.

'It's the blokes from Talimorgan. Came down to bury someone. Got a bit of a history round here. Get the locals like skittish cattle.'

The T-bones are big and juicy. The peas are sweet. Her mother says they come from a can. When Joss's father is finished he lights a cigarette and stands.

'The blokes from Talimorgan,' he says, as though it were the first line of a poem. He smiles at Joss and her mother, turns and walks into the bar. Joss and her mother go out onto the verandah. They'll listen through the window.

No children race around the car park. Instead they hang over the verandah quietly, watching the twenty tethered horses that stomp the ground. The tall boy whose father shoots roos is not there. Joss kneels up and looks through the window into the public bar. The publican hands her father a scotch. All the locals are wearing clean ironed shirts and have combed their hair. Joss knows it's because her father is going to read poems. It's a mark of respect. At the far end of the bar are the Blokes from Talimorgan. They're keeping to themselves. They order another round. The publican puts twenty beers on the bar. Joss sees one of the locals take one and begin to walk away. Before he has gone three steps a bloke from Talimorgan has him by the collar.

'Give me back me beer!' his voice is a whisper.

The publican is between them before the other bloke has a chance to say a word.

'NO thumpin' beer Charlie! Give it back!'

Charlie hands the beer back. He is a foot shorter than the bloke from Talimorgan. As he wanders back to his mates Joss hears him mutter, 'Inbreds!'

The publican gives the blokes from Talimorgan a warning and her father begins.

'We buried old Bob where the bloodwoods wave
At the foot of the Eaglehawk;'

Her father looks from the locals to the blokes from

Talimorgan. The last glass is put down on the bar. The sound of children and horses fills the silence.

'We fashioned a cross on the old man's grave
For fear that his ghost might walk;'

Her father weaves a spell on these men in the public bar. Their jaws hang open and they listen to every word and by the time he reaches the last stanza there are tears in some of the old blokes' eyes.

'We dug where the cross and the grave posts were,
We shovelled away the mould,
When sudden a vein of quartz lay bare
All gleaming with yellow gold.
'Twas a reef with never a fault nor baulk
That ran from the range's crest,
And the richest mine on the Eaglehawk
Is known as "The Swagman's Rest".'

Silence.
Her father holds the moment, before he turns and picks up his drink, and the bar erupts with applause.
'Jesus Christ mate, that was bloody good!'
'Do you know the Colt that got away?'
Her father leans across the bar his foot up on a bar stool, 'You mean *The Man from Snowy River*?'
'Yeah that's the one. Have a drink on me.'

The publican hits a glass with a fork and everyone shuts up. Her father begins again.

'There was movement at the station, for the word had passed around
That the colt from old Regret had got away,
And had joined the wild bush horses—he was worth a thousand pound,
So all the cracks had gathered to the fray.'

Joss notices another voice, a rumble, the words almost swallowed, keeping pace and rhythm with her father. It is one of the blokes from Talimorgan. Her father looks at him.

'And Clancy of the Overflow down to lend a hand,
No better horseman ever held the reins;'

Her father pauses.
The bloke from Talimorgan looks up.
Her father fixes him with a look and waits.
The bloke sips his beer and then the words come. His voice is filled with earth and wind.

'For never horse could throw him while the saddle-girths would stand—
He learnt to ride while droving on the plains.'

The corner of his mouth lifts in a smile.
Her father takes a step towards him.

'And one was there, a stripling on a small and weedy beast;
He was something like a racehorse undersized,'

The bloke from Talimorgan doesn't miss a beat.

'With a touch of Timor pony—three parts thorough-bred at least—
And such as are by mountain horsemen prized.'

All night her father and this horseman dressed in black do phrase about and keep pace with their drinks.

They leave the pub together and shake hands at the foot of the verandah. Her father swings Joss onto his back and they cross the road. The blokes from Talimorgan ride away.

Curled under a sheet on her camp stretcher in the little annex that is her bedroom, Joss drifts towards sleep, and

107

the sound of the river becomes the sound of hooves pounding across wet mountain ridges. It is the Blokes from Talimorgan, words from the poems her father recited are in the wind around them. These poems are about them. They are the Man from Ironbark and Clancy of the Overflow. They hear the voices Joss hears, the spirit whispers. But they can't find them either.

In the morning while Joss's father is packing the car and her mother is breaking camp Joss goes into the bush. She rolls in red dust and looks up at the almost white, blue sky. She can smell the sugar in her sweat. Joss has never noticed she had a smell before. In her stomach is a kind of joy, it's as big as the sky and as soft as the dust. It makes her cry.

Home again, home again . . .

The smell of coffee greets Joss as they pull up outside
the dolls' house. Tuesday: the word comes into her mind.
The Coffee Grinder in Lygon Street roasts his beans on
Tuesday. Misi jumps out the car window.

'Mischief!' screams Joss's father. 'That bloody dog.'
Her father throws open the car door. Stepping out he
hits his head.

'Jesus!

Joss knows it's not because of the dog, or because he
is too tall that her father hits his head. It's because they're
home.

Inside, he kicks at a stone that has fallen out of the
bluestone wall in the living room. 'The bloody place has
fallen apart while we've been away!'

Joss and her mother follow her father down the little
hallway into the kitchen.

'Jesus fucking Christ!'

The kitchen has tried to leave the rest of the house.
There is a huge crack between their house and next door,
two inches at the top. The house is giving her father all
the excuses he needs to be in a bad mood.

Her father tells Joss's mother to phone the fucking
landlord and storms back outside to unpack the car. Joss
looks at her mother. Her father's tone had said it was all

109

her mother's fault. Her mother says nothing. Joss hates that. She doesn't want to be a girl. She goes upstairs and climbs onto the roof.

The back bedroom window of the middle house is locked tight and the windowpanes are dirty. Joss peers in. The room is still filled with packing crates. The bald man has lived in the little house longer than Joss and her family have lived next door, but he still has a whole room of packing crates. There's no noise. He's not home; he never is, except in the morning.

Joss walks across the nail line to Judy and Roe's back bedroom window. The roof creaks. The window is open. Joss sticks her head in. Roe looks up, she is on the bed reading.

'Thought it was you. How was your holiday?'

Joss lies on the laundromat roof. People walk up and down the street. Nothing's changed.

Timmy and the Princess are stripping bricks in their backyard, in their underwear, Joss says 'hi'. They start and look embarrassed. Joss retreats back across the laundromat roof and climbs down into the lane.

The old man's in the park but Joss's father is still unpacking so she doesn't talk to him. She climbs a tree, hangs upside down and waits for her father to go inside. Unpacking the car is a production. It takes him hours. He grunts and groans and strains. The old man wanders off.

'JJ! Go and get some milk and bread from Joe's,' calls her mother from the front door.

At the milk bar Joe gives Joss an icy pole. He says it's lucky they've been away. That it's been stinking hot and all his chocolates melted.

Joss puts the milk and bread on the kitchen bench. Her mother is fiddling, her head in the oven. Her father is washing his hands again and again. No-one is saying anything but Joss thinks they have been. She goes back outside.

Lying on her stomach in the park, Joss digs a hole with a stick. She crumbles the earth in her fingers. It's soft. Not like the earth in the bush. Joss wonders where the spirits go when a city's built on top of them. Are they buried alive like feelings? And are cracks places where they try and breathe? Joss imagines the earth trying to lift the great weight of a city off its back.

That night Joss wakes from being buried alive. She is unable to breathe. Misi licks her face. Joss makes her mind stronger than her fear. Forces her lungs to let in the air. She is a warrior and she knows how to make a vaccine.

Her mother phones the landlord. He is never there. Her mother tells her father she thinks they're away.

On the first day of school, the battlelines for the year are drawn. This year there isn't Ann; there's Catherine.

Catherine talks with an American accent. She says she's met the Rolling Stones and that Mick Jagger kissed her. Joss has no idea who the Rolling Stones or Mick Jagger are. All she knows is that Catherine's uniform is too short and when she bends over, which she does all the time, you can see her underpants. They're lime-green with little bits of lace and black spots. Instinct tells Joss to keep away, like a brightly coloured fish, Catherine is dangerous.

Waiting in line, at the tuckshop at lunchtime, Catherine announces she's going to be a model. The little girl standing behind her, eager to impress, tells Catherine about Joss's friend and how she's going to be an astronaut. Catherine looks down the line at Joss's friend and gives a thin smile.

'Girls can't be astronauts,' she says.

'Of course they can,' says Joss's friend.

'No they can't.' Catherine opens a packet of Twisties and offers them to the girls around her. 'The zero gravity affects their periods and they die in space.'

Joss laughs. No-one else does. They blink and pop Twisties into their mouths. Joss's friend's face goes red. Catherine buys another packet. Joss's friend storms off. Joss follows. This year her friend will be all hers.

Maria can't mind Joss after school anymore. She has a factory job. Joss's mother hires a woman in a pink angora sweater. The woman's name is Mrs Field.

Mrs Field is waiting outside when Joss gets home from school.

'Hello dear,' she says, with a pink-painted, crooked smile. She wears the key to the dolls' house around her neck and carries a big material bag with bamboo handles.

Joss makes herself a sandwich. Mrs Field sits on the edge of a dining chair and pulls out her knitting. Joss takes her sandwich to the park.

The old man is there, sitting on a bench, looking old. He talks about winter coming. He is wearing his overcoat. Sweat beads his forehead but he doesn't notice. He asks Joss to play that flute thing of hers. He has a hankering to hear some music. Joss races inside to get the rosewood flute she stole from the chapel.

Mrs Field jumps up when Joss flies through the front door. They look at one another. Mrs Field has a tiny crystal glass in one hand and a small bottle of gin in the other. Joss runs upstairs. Mrs Field sits back down. She doesn't look up when Joss races back down the stairs two at a time and out the door.

The old man wants to hear a jig. The one that's in his head. He hums. Joss tries to follow. He snaps.

'No! No! Daaaa dada dada dada dum . . .'

By the end of the week Joss's almost got it. The old man closes his eyes and hums along.

Every afternoon at four-fifty, Mrs Field wipes her little crystal thimble, screws up her flask of gin and puts them back in her knitting-bag. Then she goes into the kitchen, fills the sink and begins to wash-up. At five o'clock, when Joss's mother comes home, Mrs Field's hands are always submerged in bubbles. If there are no dirty dishes, Mrs Field washes clean ones.

Joss doesn't like Mrs Field. She's weak. Her eyes are watery blue, all the colour bled out of them. But Mrs Field leaves Joss alone. They have an unspoken agreement. Mrs Field needs the job.

The landlord comes and looks at the crack in the kitchen wall.

Joss stands with her hands behind her back, watching, willing the crack to be unfixable. The landlord um's and ah's, scrapes some putty from the crack.

Joss and the bald man have started talking in the morning. He nods at her now when he sees her on the street.

The landlord measures the floor with a spirit level.

In the mornings the bald man's voice is thick and sad. After his shower it takes on the crispness of his day-face.

The landlord shakes his head, 'Can't fix it. The foundations have shifted.'

Joss is pleased. The crack lets in the bald man and means the dolls house isn't sealed. It's easier for Joss to breathe.

Trouble

The money is lying on Catherine's desk when Joss comes into the classroom at lunchtime to get the ball she keeps in her desk. She doesn't think about taking it, she just picks it up on her way out and goes to the tuckshop to buy chips, two icy poles and a drink. Her friend is waiting for her behind the chapel. They eat and play at being explorers. They don't hear the bell. They are the last back after lunch.

The grade four classroom's in turmoil. Everyone's talking, Catherine's crying. As Joss closes the wood and glass door behind her, the room falls silent. When she turns around everyone's looking at her. Her friend is frozen halfway across the room. Sister Beatrice grabs Joss by the arm and drags her into the middle of the room.

'I hear you had money to spend at the tuckshop today, young lady?'

'Yes Sister.'

'Where did you get it?'

'My mother gave it to me.'

'Her mother never gives her money,' squeals a girl from the back of the class.

'Christine!' snaps Sister Beatrice. The girl puts her hands on her desk and shuts up.

Joss's heart begins to beat very fast. Everyone will see she's shaking. A buzzing starts in her ears.

'How much did your mother give you?'

Joss stares blankly at Sister Beatrice.

'How much did your mother give you Jocelyn?'

'I don't know Sister. Some change from her purse.'

'And you didn't count it?' Sister Beatrice's lips are grey more than pink. She has a little moustache.

'Jocelyn I asked you a question!'

'I don't know how much money I had Sister.'

'What did you buy at the tuckshop?'

Joss goes through what she bought. Sister Beatrice writes the cost of everything on the blackboard.

'Have you any change?'

'I think so, Sister.'

'Show me.'

Joss puts her hand in her pocket. There are three coins. She thinks about only pulling one coin out but that would be dangerous. Sister Beatrice wants her to be guilty. Joss holds out thirty-five cents.

'Bring it over here.'

Joss walks across the classroom, everyone's eyes following her. Her heart isn't beating so fast anymore. The buzzing in her ears has stopped but everything looks very sharp and she hates Sister Beatrice.

'Well, well, well! Thirty-five cents plus one dollar sixty-five for what you bought makes exactly two dollars! How much did you say was taken Catherine?'

'Two dollars Sister.'

'I didn't take her money.' Joss wants to rip the saggy flesh off Sister Beatrice's cheeks, to bend her backwards and hurt her.

'Well, we'll see about that. Let's phone your mother!'

Joss's mother is busy. Joss's father comes. He hates nuns. Old women he calls hags. He rips Sister Beatrice to pieces for Joss. He calls her petty and narrow-minded in front of the Mother Superior. He quotes from the Bible, the book of David, about compassion and, without ever saying Joss had been given money, leads them to believe she had.

'Two dollars! Because the God Damn amounts are the same, that's all the proof you need. God save us from overzealous, righteous nuns. If this is the kind of logic you use it's easy to see why there was an Inquisition!' And with that Joss's father grabs her hand and drags her out of the school.

He opens the car door and literally throws her in. Joss doesn't care. Sister Beatrice has had her comeuppance and she knows her father. She can curl inside while he beats her.

He pushes her in the front door.
'I'm sorry Daddy.'
'How could you do that to me!' His eyes are white with rage. He slaps her on both sides of the face. She begins to cry.
'I'm sorry. I didn't think.'
'Those bloody righteous two-faced bitches. I won't have them thinking they're better than me.' He hits and hits. Joss curls inside. He says nothing about it being wrong to steal.

That night he hits her mother. It's her fault that Joss did this. Made him look bad.

The next day her mother doesn't go to work and Joss doesn't go to school. They don't look at each other. They watch the midday movie and eat a packet of chocolate biscuits.

The old man sees the bruises on Joss's shoulder. His old fingers trace them lightly, as though they were petals of a flower. His jaw tightens.

'I'll! . . . I'll! . . . '

He stands and starts punching the air. His legs bowing beneath him, shaky and rickety.

Spent, he sits.

Joss slides closer. Their shoulders touch. She can smell him. Old urine and bad sweat. Misi licks his hand.

That night her father comes up to tuck her in. He kisses her on the forehead and pulls the blankets up too high. He sits on the edge of her bed and looks out the window. The sky is pink and orange. The sun is setting.

'You understand. Don't you?'

Joss nods.

Her father nods. He gets up and walks out of the room.

Joss doesn't understand but she knows he wants her to.

For a few days Joss's father treads quietly. Then he forgets and things are back to normal. He tells her mother he's invited everyone back on Friday night after work for curry and carpet golf. 'You'd better get the holes fixed,' he says to her mother as he pours himself another drink. Joss buries the memory of that beating with the others, goes upstairs and climbs out onto the roof. Her stomach is tight.

In the morning when she eats, there is a sharp pain at the top of her stomach between her ribs, in the place she thinks of as her wishbone. She lies flat on her back and the pain goes.

'Pop up honey, you'll be late for school,' says her mother.

The pain becomes part of Joss, coming sometimes when she eats and other times when she's hungry. When it goes Joss forgets about it and when it comes she lies flat on her back to make it go away.

Fighting Back

Joss's mother gets a raise. There are drinks in the board-room for her. Uncle Rupert makes a speech about the great job she's doing. Joss's father raises his glass but he doesn't drink.

When they leave her father pushes her mother on the stairs. Her mother grabs hold of the banister to stop herself from falling. She looks at Joss's father.

'Don't forget who got you the job,' he whispers as he passes.

When they get home Joss's father is in a good mood. He puts on Shirley Bassey and hums along, a drink in his hand, he waits for dinner. Joss's mother is silent. She cooks and serves and eats and then reaches across the table to clear the plates

'Come here, sexy legs,' Joss's father grabs Joss's mother by the wrist. Her mother snaps his grip and holds his stare. Joss doesn't move a muscle. She thinks of red dogs and gutting fish. Her mother is fighting back. The dining room seems very small.

Sex is something that happens to you when you grow up. Joss doesn't see the big deal. Little girls whisper

118

about it in the chapel while the priest raises the eucharist to the crucified image of Christ.

'It goes hard and they stick it in you.'

'In the name of the Father, Son and Holy Ghost.'

'Really? Have you ever seen one?'

'The body and blood of Our Lord Jesus Christ.'

'Get out! But me sister has. They get huge she says.'

The choir starts singing and the little girls sweet voices join the rest of the school.

'Let us sing a song of joy for men shall love each other . . .'

Joss knows sex is about sweat and strength. Men are stronger than women. When her mother fights back the night noises are louder. Her father is stronger. He always gets what he wants.

Joss is faster than the boys at the housing commission flats and quicker. She can out-run and out-climb them. She can hurl their soccer ball onto a factory roof and be gone before they realize what's happened. All they have is strength. She has wit. It's a private game, like commando training.

The nights get colder. Joss lays kindling on the fire.

'Mum where's the . . .'

Whack.

'Don't call your mother "Mum".' Joss's father has her by the hair. 'Alright?'

Joss nods, a small movement felt by his hand. He kisses her on the forehead. Her father loves her.

'Got a story for me?' he asks.

'Two peas in a pod,' she says. She wants him to be happy. He smiles. His lips disappear under his moustache and he softens back into the creases of his face. Joss sits on his lap and fiddles with the buttons on his shirt:

119

'Once upon a time,' Joss knows how to begin a story, 'there were two peas lost and alone in a broad bean patch. Each pea thought it was the only one of its kind in the whole world and that something was wrong with it. Both wanted so much to be like the big, juicy broad beans. But every time one of them tried to crawl into a pod to get away from the cold, windy weather, they were kicked out because they were so small and embarrassing to have around.

'All winter the peas rolled around the field trying to find a bean plant that would have them. But no-one would. It was a very cold winter and the peas began to shrivel and shrink and loose all their strength.

'Finally, blown together in the middle of the broad bean patch by an icy cold wind, the two peas found each other. They didn't speak. They just sort of cuddled. And then the snow came.

' "So alike," whispered one of the peas to the other as they were buried.

'The next spring in the middle of the broad bean patch was a sweet pea vine. It didn't get any bugs and the peas were sugar-sweet. And in each pod were two peas.

' "Just two," said the farmer to his wife, "In every pod two peas exactly the same." '

Her father looks down, 'Exactly the same eh?'

'Like my friend and me. That's what Sister calls us. Two peas in a pod.'

Her father snorts a laugh and pushes her off his knee.

He pours himself a drink. Her father has his back to her. He sculls and pours himself another. Joss goes and lights the fire. The flames are blue from the ink in the newspaper. Joss watches them, her heart is hurting.

'Done your homework, honey?' asks her mother from the foot of the stairs.

'Didn't have any.'

'Bedtime then, eh.'

It is six-fifteen. The black dog is stirring. Joss goes and cleans her teeth.

When Joss comes back into the lounge room her father is standing, poised in front of the television, drink in hand. Joss looks at the screen, it's the ABC news.

'Good night Daddy.'

'Jesus fucking Christ!' her father sips, shakes his head in disgust and sits, 'What the hell does this bloody government think it's doing.'

Joss goes to bed. It takes her a long time to get to sleep, her ears won't rest. They listen even when she doesn't want to. Finally the gentle rasp of Misi's breathing draws her into sleep.

In the morning, Joss cleans up the broken glass on the kitchen floor and a few drops of blood in the bathroom. She notices them when she's sitting on the loo. They're on the side of the sink. Her mother mustn't have seen them. The light in the bathroom isn't very good.

Joss hears the bald man turn on his kitchen tap. He's filling his kettle.

'Morning,' she calls through the crack.

'Mor . . .,' his voice breaks. He coughs and tries again, 'Morning.'

'Sleep well?'

'No. Not really. You?' He puts the kettle on the stove and lights the gas. Joss can hear him.

'No. Bad dreams.' Joss jumps up and sits on the bench. She peels a banana and leans back against the wall with the crack.

'Umm, bad dreams,' he says, she hears him put his cup on a saucer and open the fridge.

Joss's mother comes down the stairs. She is already

dressed. Her face looks alright. She's wearing long sleeves. The cut must be on her arm.

'Your father was going to drive you to school this morning but he's still asleep.' Her mother smiles a shrug and puts the kettle on. Joss hears the bald man turn on the shower.

'That's alright.'

Joss and her mother walk as far as the tram stop together.

'See you tonight, honey. Have a good day.'

'Bye.' Joss keeps walking up the hill. Her mother waits for the city tram. Her mother is never late for work and she is always home before Joss's father. She makes sure the house is shipshape and gets dinner ready before he gets home. That's how Joss knows her mother likes her job. She is careful not to give him a reason to tell her to quit.

April

All day, Joss has that pain in her stomach. She lies on the floor in the toilet at school. It doesn't go away. After school she cooks herself custard from a packet before going to the park. At first the custard tastes sweet but then it's sort of bitter. She puts the saucepan in the sink for Mrs Field to wash.

It's drizzling. No-one's in the park. Joss climbs the old elm opposite the dolls' house. Her fingers find holds in the bark and she squeezes her toes into the scars where there should have been branches. The council doesn't like children climbing their trees. Last spring the council men came and took away the tree-house she was building. They even took away her fish bowl. But they couldn't take away the trees. Joss pulls her knees to her chest and sits in the heart of the tree.

She leans her cheek against the bark, like a lover. Things are stirring in her. This year she'll be eleven. Her father is always unhappy now. He sweats at night and only laughs when there are people round. If her mother tries to be happy her father hits her and tells her to shut up. Joss's eyes wander to the other end of the park. She sees the old man on the wrong bench. He is lying down and has his coat pulled around him. He never sits at that end of the park. He says there's too much traffic. She watches him. A red car honks at an old woman dressed in black crossing the road. The old woman ignores the red car and keeps on walking. The driver leans out his window and yells something. The old woman goes into the church opposite the park, opposite the old man, who doesn't move.

Something is wrong. The pain in Joss's stomach sharpens. She leaps down out of the tree and begins to run towards the old man. Joss tries to lift him. He is heavy. The wind is cold. Her fingers get caught in his hair. He is bleeding from a wound on the side of his head. She needs to get help. She needs to be here with him. Panic. She cannot be in two places at once. Not in real life. Joss takes off her jumper. She rests the old man's head on it. It has the smell of her. She runs. It's three blocks to the police station.

'Come! Quick! Please. He's hurt!'

'Who love? Who?'

'The old man in the park. He's bleeding.' Joss begins to cry now because she can, because the policemen will help her. She looks at them and waits for them to come. They don't pick up their hats. The two younger officers smile at each other and go back to their bookwork. Even the sergeant is smiling. Joss doesn't understand.

'OK love, which park?' asks the Sergeant.

'McArthur Place.'

The sergeant writes it down.

'Aren't you coming?'

'We'll see what we can do. You run along home now, little one.'

Suddenly Joss understands. She would like to smash their faces in. She runs from the police station.

Joss is out of breath when she gets back to the old man. He hasn't moved. Her jumper has his blood on it. Joss uses all her strength to lift him. She's a little bit rough. She slides in beside him and rests his head on her lap. He doesn't even know she's there. She tries to hum the jig he likes. The tune gets stuck in her throat.

The streetlights come on and it begins to get dark. Joss can feel the rain running down the back of her neck. She begins to talk to the old man. About the sun and gutting fish. She talks about small things that are the right size for happiness.

Joss doesn't know what the time is when the police divi van arrives. All she knows is that it's dark and the policemen are angry that she didn't go home. They lift the old man roughly from Joss's arms. She tries to hold onto him. They tell her not to be silly. Joss thought the police would be like the police in her father's show. They're not. She has handed the old man over to them. She has betrayed him.

They lie him down in the back of the divi van and shut the door.

'Where do you live?'

Joss cannot answer. She cannot breathe. The young constable takes her arm. Joss kicks him and runs. He follows. She bangs on the door of the dolls' house. Her mother opens the door. A grey, worried face against bright light.

'Oh JJ!'

Her father appears in the doorway. 'Where the hell have you been?' The constable appears behind Joss. Her father pulls right back. Her mother lifts her up and takes her inside. Her father talks with the policeman.

Inside Mrs Field is weeping. 'Oh Jocelyn why didn't you tell me where you were?' Joss wants to scream at her, because you're a gin-soaked old bitch!

Her mother takes her upstairs. Dries her. Wraps her in a blanket and sits with her on the bed. 'Well?'

'There was an old man in the park. He was sick.' Joss feels her chest tightening. No, she won't cry.

Joss looks at her mother. 'I couldn't leave him.'

Her mother knows by her eyes it's the truth. She puts her arm around her and rocks her, gentle.

In the morning, Joss's mother makes her French toast.

Her father storms down the stairs.

Joss stands up.

'Where the fuck are they?' Her father can't find his glasses, he's late for work. But really he's angry with her.

'I'm sorry Daddy.' The words spill out. 'I'll never do it again.'

He stops and looks at her.

Joss swallows. She didn't mean to make trouble.

'Make sure you don't.'

'I will.'

After breakfast Joss cuts her hair. Her father likes it short.

Joss's friend decides they should join the basketball team.

'No!' says Joss.

'Why not? What's wrong with you?'

'Nothing's wrong with me. It's you!' Joss walks away. Her friend follows.

'Me? What have I done?'

Joss turns on her, 'Go play with your stupid little friends and their stupid little ball then.'

'You're so up yourself.'

Joss hits out. Her friend hits back. There is release in hitting out. In clawing. Once she is hurt she will cry.

The old man doesn't come back. Joss leaves money in the lane for him. She leaves a blanket and a pair of her father's shoes. It rains and they rot.

Winter

Winter wraps itself around the tension in the dolls' house. At night rain blankets the sounds of her father's anger. Heavy drops, drowning the words he yells at her mother before they can leave the house. Some things are private. And then when he sleeps the rain washes away the echo of him, with its constant rhythm, making it easier to pretend in the morning.

Joss doesn't know what's happened to take the steely grey from her mother's blue eyes. She doesn't understand the concern in the way her mother hands her father his cup of tea each morning as though nothing had happened. She tries to help her mother by being good. But it's not easy. If she says 'can I leave the table' instead of 'may I leave the table', she gets the back of his hand. Her father is always ready to snap. Sometimes when he looks at her, Joss imagines she can see the black dog snarling, dark shadows and white teeth in her father's green eyes.

Her father is always tired. He complains about everything, their life, his job, headaches. And it's always her mother's fault. Her father takes his Disprin with brandy, 'Who needs water, fish fuck in it.'

'I'm worried about him Clair.' Uncle Rupert's rumbling

127

voice rolls around the little lounge room. Joss sits on the landing at the top of the stairs and listens. Her father is working late. Uncle Rupert has come to talk to her mother.

'So am I.'

'It's affecting his work. I tried to talk to him about it.'

'And?'

'He stormed out.'

Silence.

'How is he at home Clair? Come on, family, remember.'

A car speeds past, wheels screeching at the corner.

'Difficult,' says her mother with a laugh to make Uncle Rupert think he knows. It works. Uncle Rupert rocks back in the big black armchair, a knowing smile on his face.

'Another drink?'

'Why not.'

Her mother takes his glass and leaves the room. Joss watches Uncle Rupert rock back and forth, the chair squeaking under his weight, as he thinks and taps his thumbs together. Just as her mother comes back into the lounge room he looks up and says, 'I think he should see a doctor, have a check-up.' Joss's mother laughs and as she lifts her head spies Joss at the top of the stairs.

'Go to bed young lady, now!' There's no humour in her mother's look. Joss has overstepped the line.

In the morning Joss finds her father asleep in the lounge room, the brandy bottle curled under his arm. Joss goes and has a bath. When she comes out her mother is up and her father is sitting at the dining-room table staring into his tea. The bags under his eyes are swollen. Joss looks at her mother, her mother turns away, she won't meet Joss's eye.

Joss goes upstairs. She picks up her flute from beside her bed and climbs out onto the roof. She goes to her corner. She misses the old man. She begins to play his jig. She imagines him in the lane, listening. She plays the jig over and over. Suddenly the window behind her flies open and Roe sticks her head out.

'That's lovely Joss. But do you think you could play in your room?'

Lying in bed that night Joss can hear the murmur of her parents, talking. They're in the kitchen. She hears her father move through the house. Hears the sound of glass against glass. Her father is pouring himself a drink in the lounge room now. He has a heavy hand these days.

'Richard, I'm worried about you.' Her mother's voice is soft like butter. Her mother has followed him into the lounge room. 'Richard?'

Her father doesn't answer. Joss hears the big black chair squeak. He's sat down.

'Please? For me.'

'For you! Everything I do is for you.'

Her mother doesn't answer. The chair squeaks. Her father steps across the room.

'Isn't it?'

'Please Richard, don't.'

'Well isn't it?'

'Richard, that's not the point.'

'Yes or no.'

'Yes! Yes! But—'

Whack. Something falls. A chair. Her mother. Silence.

'For God's sake get up. You look bloody stupid.'

It was her mother.

The television goes on. It's Graham Kennedy. Her father laughs. He's pouring himself another drink. Joss never relaxes her body. Not even in bed. She sleeps with clenched fists.

The days wind tighter into the nights, tighter and tighter. Joss is always listening.

Things That Go
Bump In the Night

Sounds with no edges only weight, burr into Joss's skull, until she wakes. The pillow is wet. She's been crying. Thud. Something hard is cushioned. It's dark. Muffled sounds.

Joss is on the landing now. It wasn't her it was her feet. Her heart is beating very fast. The sounds come. Choked words.

'Dooon't pleeeease.'

'I'll fucking do what I like with you.'

Joss is somewhere between sleep and wake. Peer in through the little window above the stairs. Quiet now. There's a voice in her head.

The lamp is on in her parent's bedroom. Dull yellow light. Shadows. Joss sees but doesn't understand. Her mother is tied to the bed. Her father has something in his hand. He is over her mother.

'Open your fucking mouth.'

Joss's mother clenches her jaw and pulls her head back. Her father hits her mother and grabs her by the hair. He makes her open her mouth. Joss doesn't understand. Her mother screams but the sound is choked because her father has that thing in her mother's mouth. His arm pulls back. They are pliers in his hand. Her mother is screaming now, really screaming. Her father leans over her. Pushing his weight into her mother's mouth. Suddenly Joss understands. Her father is pulling out her mother's teeth.

'NOooo . , .' Joss is sick on the stairs.

'What the . . .' Her father stumbles towards the bedroom door. Joss runs.

'You fuckin' little bitch!' The pliers bounce off the bluestone wall behind her. Joss flies out the front door and into the park. She scrambles up her tree, as high as she can go and hides among the leaves.

Her father throws open the front door of the dolls' house. He is a black shadow in the doorway.

'You fucking little whore! Slut!'

Her heart is beating. She can taste brandy.

'Run away from me, you little bitch! I'll show you!' He slams the door.

The sound of things breaking and a ranting blur of words come from the dolls' house. Then silence.

After a long time, her parents' bedroom light goes off. And then a light downstairs comes on. No noise, just light. It's her mother. Joss climbs down out of the tree. She is shaking and cuts herself. It's cold. She's not climbing very well. Joss goes into the back lane. The back gate is locked. Joss has to climb it.

The light in the bathroom is on. Joss walks across the garden. Her feet are dirty. She stops at the back door. She can hear her mother running water. She looks into the bathroom, through the crack between the blind and the window frame. Her mother is pouring salt into a glass. There is blood on her hand. Joss thinks of the tooth fairy.

She walks back through the garden and climbs up onto the roof. She doesn't want to see anyone. She just wants her dog.

Joss hears Misi come into her room and jump on the

bed. She leans in the window and clicks her fingers. Misi comes. Joss lifts her out onto the roof. Her bed's not safe.

The back door opens. 'Joss?' Her mother's voice is a whisper. A soft smudge.

'Here Mum.'

'Umm,' says her mother. A small sound. There aren't any words. Her mother sits on the back doorstep.

Joss stays on the roof.

Her father wakes with a hangover. Joss hears him stumble from the bedroom. He slams the bathroom door. Joss hears him throwing up. The toilet flushes. The shower goes on. He is in the bathroom a long time. Her mother is inside, somewhere. Joss pushes back into a corner of the roof. She can hear the traffic building up. People going to work. Buses stop, heavy. Heavier, they edge their way back into the traffic.

The front door slams shut. Her father's car starts. She listens till the sound of it disappears into the traffic.

She stands. Her legs are stiff. She climbs in her bedroom window. Pulls Misi in after her.

Her mother hears Joss on the stairs, she disappears into the bathroom and closes the door. Joss moves about the kitchen. She needs something hot.

'You better hurry. Or you'll be late for school. I told your father you'd already gone.'

Joss leans her cheek against the bathroom door, 'OK Mum.'

Her mother doesn't want to see her.

'I love you,' whispers Joss.

Her mother begins to cry.

Joss hears the bald man in his kitchen. He doesn't say good morning. He has heard everything. Joss is ashamed.

She goes upstairs, slips her school uniform, with its Peter Pan collar, over her head. She pulls white socks over her dirty feet and combs her hair. Her shoes are scuffed. Her school bag smells of rotten bananas. She empties it in the kitchen.

'Bye Mum.'

'Bye.'

Joss hates her father.

'Will you pay attention girl!' Sister's ruler comes down hard on Joss's desk. Joss comes back.

'Sorry Sister.'

'It's not good enough, Jocelyn. It's just not good enough.'

Joss feels nothing. At lunchtime she goes into the chapel. She hides in the confessional. She doesn't want to see anyone.

'Where were you?' Her friend is pissed off. Joss shrugs.

When Joss gets home, Mrs Field is not there and the front door is open. Joss goes inside. Her mother calls from the bedroom.

'I'm just having a little lie down.'

Her father doesn't come home and her mother doesn't leave the bedroom. Joss cooks herself tinned spaghetti. Uncle Rupert rings to see how her mother is. Joss says her mother's sleeping.

'Best thing. Best thing,' says Uncle Rupert. 'Those bloody dentists can be absolute barbarians. You tell your mother to take care of herself.'

'I will.' Joss hangs up the phone. Her mother's a good liar.

Joss leaves to go to school the next morning, but she never gets there. She wanders. When she gets home, her mother is in the kitchen. Most of the swelling has gone down. The bruises are covered with make-up. There are scones and jam and cream on the dining-room table and Joss can smell a roast cooking.

'How was school?' Her mother can't smile yet.

'OK.'

Her mother goes back to shelling peas. Joss goes upstairs. She takes out her knife and begins to carve a turtle out of a piece of sandy stone she brought home from the bush. The light begins to go. Joss hears her father's car pull up. She closes her bedroom door and begins to sing. 'A sailor went to sea, sea, sea, to see what he could see, see, see but all that he could see, see, see was the bottom of the deep blue sea, sea, sea . . .'

There's a knock on her door.

'Joss, dinner.' It's her mother.

Joss puts down her turtle and her knife. She goes downstairs. In the middle of the table are pink rosebuds. Her father has bought them for her mother.

'Gravy?' asks her mother.

Joss nods. She eats everything on her plate one after another. Beans first. Potatoes, pumpkin, meat, peas. Then she asks if she may be excused. Upstairs she sticks her head out the window and her finger down her throat. She puts Misi on the roof to eat up the mess.

Joss leaves in the morning before her parents get up. She goes to bed before her father comes home. She will not speak to him. On Friday night he brings everyone back after work. Joss hears them pour through the door at about ten.

'Clair you poor bitch! Fucking wisdom teeth.'

'Had to happen sometime Barry.'

They've all swallowed the story. Maybe even her mother has. Joss hates them all. They all think her father's wonderful. And he's not. He's not. Joss cries herself to sleep.

And dreams the strengths she will need for the next

day. Each one, she places in her leather pouch and careful not to spill them, climbs the wooden ladder back to reality.

Her mother heals. She goes back to work. Everyone pretends nothing has happened. Her mother, her father, the neighbours. Joss can't.

Her father stops her on the stairs.

'What's wrong? Talk to me.' He's trying to be gentle. Her silence is driving him crazy. Good. She wants to hurt him.

Her mother comes up behind him; she doesn't want trouble.

Standing two stairs up Joss can look straight into her father's eyes. 'I hate you,' she says and holds his look. He begins to cry. Joss tightens the bindings of her armour. He closes his eyes. Joss pushes past him. She picks up her school bag and walks out the front door.

That afternoon, when Joss walks out the school gate, her mother is waiting for her. She has a bag of hot jam donuts. They walk home through the park.

'JJ, I need you to help me.' Joss looks at her mother and licks the sugar off her lips.

'It's not him, Joss. He's sick.'

Her mother's eyes are pleading, 'Please. He is trying.'

Joss tries to tighten the bindings of her armour. She looks away. But this is her mother.

'He's not drinking as much. And he's going to see a doctor. For the headaches. That's why he snaps.'

Joss kicks at a stick. Her mother touches her arm, 'Please Joss. Help me. If we can be a family . . .'

Joss hadn't meant to make it worse.

'I'm sorry, Mum.'

'Don't be.' Her mother puts her arm around Joss and kisses her on the head.

'Another donut?' Her mother is trying to jolly things up. Joss shakes her head. She's not hungry.

Joss goes to bed before her father comes home. There is a moon and a wind. Shadows move across her bedroom ceiling. Joss has a feeling she has done something wrong. Her father comes home. She hears him on the stairs. She shuts her eyes.

'Little mouse?' Her father pokes his head into her room. 'You awake?'

Joss doesn't move. He sits on the bed and begins to stroke her head. She makes a little noise and turns, like she would if she were asleep. Joss is a good actor.

'I love you,' he whispers. He pats Misi and leaves.

Joss opens her eyes. It begins to rain. Big drops on the tin roof outside her bedroom window. Joss drags Misi in under the covers.

Playing at family

The next morning Joss bounces down the stairs.

'Morning Daddy.'

Her father puts down his paper.

'Morning little mouse.'

She smiles at him and goes to make herself breakfast. Her mother is making a shopping list. They are going to the market.

'Your father's idea,' says her mother. Her mother is saying that her father is trying. Joss smiles. I'm trying too, Mummy.

They move through the colour and people. A mother, a father and a child. A dog on a lead. A happy family. Her father stops. He buys hot chestnuts.

'Have one. Go on. They're beautiful.'

Uncertain, the child bites into the sweet nut. She likes it. Her mother laughs. Joss is watching herself from outside. She has given them her smile and gone where they can't find her. She is watching and waiting for her father to snap.

When they get home Joss takes some salami and bread and climbs up onto the laundromat roof. She sits with her legs dangling over the edge and watches the people on the street. She watches them like she watched herself at the market, from above. Alone, all the pieces of her fit together. It's when she's with other people, with her father that they don't.

For the next few months there is a kind of peace in the dolls' house. Her father takes little pink tablets in the morning and brown ones in the evening. Traditions are started. Friday night movie with takeaway Chinese. The market on Saturday. Chocolate cake and footy on Sunday. Joss watches it all from outside.

She watches herself acting out a little girl's excitement at catching a tram all the way to St Kilda. At seeing the sea flat and greyish.

'It's not much of a sea.' Joss joins herself with that comment.

Her father laughs. Joss pulls away again.

She watches herself open her eyes wide for her father, when they enter the dining room of the Crystal Ball Room.

'Oh Daddy! It's beautiful,' she says and slides her new black patent leather shoes over the thick maroon carpet. Her father says something but Joss is caught in the thought of how good she is getting at this.

She takes her cues from her parents, who take theirs from the surroundings and the waiters. They talk and laugh. The concierge comes up and compliments her father on his beautiful family, his beautiful child.

'One child with those eyes, is worth six,' he says. Her father laughs. Joss has her father's eyes.

Joss lowers her fingers into the warm lemon water of the fingerbowl that comes with the whole roast duck, drowning in orange sauce. Joss almost joins herself then. She likes the idea of bathing her fingers at the table, but her father leans over and sticks his hand into the bowl.

'You're supposed to squeeze the lemon,' he says,

destroying the perfect lemon circles with his thick fingers.

'It cuts the grease.' He smiles. He looks stupid. He's been darkening his moustache.

Her mother puts on weight. She even begins to show Joss's father small signs of affection.

'It's going to be alright JJ,' her mother says one morning over toast and marmalade. 'It really is.'

Joss feels nothing. She is still waiting, watching from above herself, from above the dolls' house.

The problem with not being inside herself is that Joss gets lost and can't find the way back. Sometimes she'd like to.

On Sundays, she watches herself scream at the television with her father.

'Come on you bastards! What's wrong with you?' Then licking the chocolate cake from her fingers, she hears herself say, 'I don't know Daddy. They just haven't got it together.' And her father laughs and wraps his arms around her, not even noticing that it isn't her anymore. That the little girl never looks at him. Not like before, with love.

Her father has an allergic reaction to the little brown tablets. The doctor changes them. Now he takes red ones at night.

Her mother phones Aurora in Sydney. Joss kneels on the stairs drawing horses heads, listening.

'He seems almost happy Aurora . . . Yeah, I know you said it would but . . . He's still tired . . . No, work's going well. Don't suppose you'd be interested in coming down . . . It's a beautiful script . . . Two weeks' time . . . That's wonderful! Six months . . . Guess I'll just have to find you something else later in the year . . . Yeah, yeah I will . . . Me? Happy? Almost . . . '

Joss scribbles over her drawings. She doesn't want to listen anymore. There are pictures in her head. She goes outside. Bad pictures of her father. She kicks up clumps of dirt and grass.

At school Joss steals money from the offering box. She wants to get into trouble but no-one catches her. Joss and her friend start playing a new game, photographer and model. It makes Joss feel strange. She has a sense it's wrong. But she doesn't say anything. Neither does her friend. They just keep playing it. If they get caught, if someone says something, they can pretend they didn't know, even to each other.

Her father comes home one night very tired and shaky. Her mother says there's a nasty flu going round and sends him to bed. She makes him chicken soup and toast.

At eight-thirty he calls out, 'Down!'

Joss's mother races to the bedroom. Joss follows. Her father is sitting up, his eyes are open, but he is asleep. He's dreaming.

'Down!' he says again and gestures with his hand. He is worried, he is frowning.

Her mother is gentle with him. 'Yes, that's right, lie down.'

Joss watches from the door.

Her mother tucks her father in. She brushes the hair back off his face and kisses his forehead lightly. Joss's stomach tightens and then the pain comes in the place she thinks of as her wishbone. Joss puts herself to bed.

In the morning her father is fine. He is hungry and eats three eggs.

Leaf buds begin to swell on the old elms in the park. The ice thaws from the wind in waves of spring rain. Joss's father is still behaving himself. He hasn't hit her mother. He hasn't even kicked the dog in nearly three months.

Her mother is always tender towards her father now. At night when they watch television her mother rubs her father's feet. She runs baths for him and cooks him special things to eat. He buys her mother flowers and holds her hand. Joss watches from outside. She misses her daddy. Sometimes she wants to say, I didn't mean it Daddy, I don't hate you. But then she feels uneasy and the pain comes. Inside she feels something is wrong. What Joss knows is the black dog; he's only behaving because she doesn't trust him, and as soon as she does, he'll snap, like a trap.

Small hands

Joss's father is given a week off work. No-one tells her why.

She wakes up one Monday morning to find him in the kitchen cooking them all kippers for breakfast and making her lunch, liverwurst sandwiches. Her mother steps out of the bathroom. Her father flips the kippers. Her mother and father kiss. Her mother is dressed for work. Her father is in his silk dressing-gown with little anchors. He is wearing a cravat. Joss's mother smiles and sips her tea, she has lipstick on her teeth. Joss feels uncomfortable, like someone is teasing her.

In English, Joss writes a story about losing her cat. She is missing the old man. Sister makes her read it out to the class and then goes through each word Joss has misspelt and each punctuation error.

'Ankle. A, N, C, U, L.'

Catherine begins to titter. Joss wants to punch her in the face.

'It's all very well to have an imagination, Jocelyn. But if no-one can decipher your spelling, what's the point.' Sister marks Joss's paper with a big red four out of ten. Catherine gets nine out of ten for her story 'My Holiday to Disneyland.'

At lunchtime, on the asphalt playground, Joss runs backwards into Catherine and knocks her flying. Catherine takes all the skin off her knees.

'You!'

'What? I didn't see you. I was running backwards!'

Catherine is ushered off to the infirmary by a group of cooing grade-fours. The Sister in the infirmary cuts the knees out of Catherine's nylon stockings to apply Mercurochrome. Catherine is quiet for the rest of the afternoon. Joss is satisfied.

When Joss gets home her father is sleeping in the big black chair. The house is clean and there are pink rosebuds on the dining-room table. Joss reads the card beside them: 'To my beautiful and patient wife. You are the best thing in my life. Richard'. Joss takes an apple from the fruit bowl and goes upstairs. She climbs out onto the roof and walks across the wall to the laundromat. She looks down onto the main street. There's an old woman dressed in black pushing a vinyl shopping trolley and three boys from the flats. Joss drops her apple core just behind the boys, then ducks.

For dinner, her mother serves up steak and kidney pie. It's her father's favourite. Joss hates it. Joss moves the bits of kidney around her plate with her fork.

'It's your birthday on Sunday,' says her father.

Joss looks up.

'What do you want to do?'

She's all there. He's remembered her birthday. It's like someone has opened a window in a room that's been boarded up.

'Could, could my friend come over?' she asks.

'I think we could manage that,' says her father and laughs. 'But how about a special birthday dinner on Friday night. Just us.'

Joss nods and breathes her smile in, filling her lungs.

On the way to school Joss practises all the different ways she can invite her friend over. 'It's my birthday on Sunday: Want to come over?'; 'If you're not doing anything on Sunday thought you might like to come over. It's my birthday'. In the end Joss simply tells her friend that she's coming over Sunday and that her mother has to say yes because it's her birthday. Her friend doesn't seem to mind Joss's bossy invitation. They sit on the steps of the chapel planning all the things they can do. Go roller-skating, buy hot jam donuts, maybe even go up to Lygon Street by themselves. The two girls lean forward and pull up their socks at the same time. They look at each other and link little fingers.

'Shakespeare.'

'Browning.'

They laugh. They never jinx.

That night after dinner, while her mother is doing the dishes, Joss's father tells her a story about a child lost in the forest and found by sparrows, small birds that cannot lift the child and so pull out their own feathers to cover him and keep him warm. How the sparrows make the child theirs, teaching him where to find water and berries and how to play. And how one day, when the child is bigger and can run like a deer through the forest, a man sees him and chases him. Wanting to take back what is his. But the child does not belong to the man and when the man corners him on the edge of a cliff the child spreads his arms and gives himself to the wind like the sparrows.

The next night after dinner her father says he has another story for her. Joss sits cross-legged in front of the fire and her father tells her a story about a smart young boy who falls in with the wrong crowd and becomes a donkey in their circus. It's a funny story. Her father acts out all the parts, makes his hair stand up like ears and his moustache droop down like Chinese whiskers. Joss laughs till she cries.

In the morning, as her mother kisses her father goodbye, Joss wonders when her father will get sick of being home during the day alone. He always wants her mother there. Even when he's fishing and doesn't talk to her, he wants her there. But that night he says he likes this not-working business and that he and the dog are becoming quite good friends.

After dinner he tells Joss a story about a boy who eats a bad pill and does all the things he knows he shouldn't. How everyone begins to hate him and chases him away. Until one day, on the furthest edge of the world, he meets a simple girl who doesn't beat him when he breaks her eggs. She listens when he tells her about the pill, and suggests he try to cough it up. She finds herbs and mixes potions, until in his sleep one night the boy coughs up the pill and is himself again.

By Thursday Joss and her friend are bursting with excitement about seeing each other out of school. Her friend has organized her mother to drop her off at ten.

On Thursday night her father tells her the story of the little mouse.

'You're my little mouse,' he says and kisses her forehead.

Joss feels sad when she goes to bed. She doesn't know why. She listens in the dark for small sounds. There aren't any. Her parents go to bed early. Her father snores.

On Friday morning her father is still asleep when Joss and her mother leave. They close the front door quietly behind them. Joss steps on cracks all the way to school.

That afternoon when Joss comes out of school, her

father is standing at the school gate. He waves. He looks smaller than she thinks of him.

At the lights he takes her hand. They cross to the park. Sunlight filters through the new green leaves of the trees. Neither of them says anything. Joss feels the smallness of her hand in his. The sureness of it.

They step out of the park, cross the black bitumen road and wander down the footpath. Past the old pink and blue houses of peeling paint, with their tiny concrete front yards and their neat flowerbeds of dahlias or roses.

Joss looks at her father. He has never picked her up from school before. She has a sense she should remember this.

Snap

'Happy Birthday little mouse,' her father lifts his glass. He has taken them to a French restaurant. He has ordered for them, frogs' legs and snails. Her father looks at her mother. 'She's growing up isn't she?' he says. Her mother nods.

The snails come in a cloud of garlic steam. Her mother shows Joss how to hold the shell in the special clamp and work the snail out with the little fork. Joss loses a snail across the table, she and her mother laugh. Her father is sweating. He wipes his brow.

'Daddy . . .' Joss looks at him. All the colour has gone from his face. She forgets what she was about to say.

'I just need to lie down for a bit. You stay and finish.'

Her father leaves the restaurant.

Joss and her mother sit there. Nothing like this has ever happened before. Her father is never small about being sick. He is never small about anything. The baked fish arrives. They can't eat it. They're not hungry.

Joss's mother looks at her. 'Do you mind?' she asks.

'No,' says Joss, standing up and putting her napkin on the table. Something's shifted. She wants to go home.

The waiter thinks they're leaving because the food was bad. 'No! No!,' says Joss's mother. 'It's not the food. Please.' Joss is already out the door.

It's two and a half blocks from the restaurant to the dolls' house. At the corner the lights turn yellow. Joss's mother grabs her by the wrist and dashes across the road. They both keep running, slowing down to a fast walk only when they turn the corner to the dolls' house.

Inside, Joss's father is curled on the bed in the dark, his knees pulled up to his chest. Joss stands at the foot of her parents' bed. Her mother wipes the sweat from her father's brow.

'It's just the flu,' he mutters.

'Mmm. It's just the flu,' repeats her mother. Her father begins to shake. Her mother pulls a blanket over him.

'Get me some Disprin and make your father a cup of tea.'

Joss does what she is told.

The Disprin doesn't work and her mother can't make her father drink the tea. His face has gone soft like a child's. He begins to shake again.

'We're going to the hospital,' says her mother in a voice that defies panic. 'Call a taxi.'

Her mother wraps her father in a brown-and-red checked blanket. It takes her a long time to get him down the stairs. The taxi honks outside the dolls' house. Joss opens the front door. Her mother gets her father to the taxi. They get in the back. Joss gets in the front.

'Which hospital, love,' asks the taxidriver.

'I don't know,' says Joss.

'The closest,' says her mother from the back.

The taxidriver takes them to St Vincent's, down the road from Joss's school, opposite the big park.

Joss pays the taxi with money out of her mother's purse. A man dressed in white helps her mother get her father from the taxi into the hospital.

Inside, it is very bright. They put her father on a trolley. Her mother holds her father's hand. Doctors and nurses all dressed in white look at her father and talk to her mother. Joss keeps out of their way and holds onto her mother's purse. Her mother looks over her shoulder to check that Joss is there. They begin to wheel her father down the corridor. Her mother keeps hold of her father's hand and walks along beside him. Joss follows.

They go up in an elevator, along a bare corridor that leads to swinging double doors. The men push the doors open and wheel her father through. The nurse turns and smiles at Joss. 'You'll wait here won't you dear. There's a good girl.' There are padded benches lining the wall. The doors swing shut.

Joss sits down. She puts her mother's purse on the bench beside her. She sits on her hands and stares at the floor. The lino in the corridor is cream with green flecks. Joss doesn't feel anything. She stares at a square of lino until the green flecks begin to move across the cream tile and make little patterns. Time stops for Joss. She notices the dust in the corners by the double doors. The grey chewing gum under the bench opposite. The way the lights from the traffic on the street below move down the hallway. That all the nurses feet look the same. They wear white shoes with thick soles and laces. The double doors open. Joss looks up. Her mother tries to smile. She's been crying.

'Do you want to say goodnight to Daddy?'

Joss follows her mother through the double doors and into a small, dimly-lit room. There's a plastic tent around her father and tubes going into his nose and arm. Her father lies back on four pillows in a big metal cot. His face is melting. He tries to smile. Joss rests her hand on the side of the cot. There's a thought on the edge of her consciousness; she clamps it down. Think things and they happen.

'Goodnight Daddy,' she says. 'See you in the morning.'

He doesn't speak. Joss knows he can't. Joss puts her small hand over his. His hand is cold. She smiles, defying the panic in her gut, she feels like her mother. She looks into his eyes. He's still inside. Behind the cool green.

'I love you,' she whispers. He looks at her. His eyes say, Little mouse. Hers say, I don't hate you.

Her mother takes her hand. They leave the little room. The double doors swing shut behind them. Walking away, down the corridor to the elevator, her mother squeezes her hand. Strong she is saying, strong. Her mother pushes the button and keeps her eyes on the elevator doors. Joss copies her. She doesn't look back.

They walk out through Casualty, with its fluorescent lights, into the night. On the corner by the park there are taxis. They climb into the back of one and go home.

Her mother makes tea. It's the witching hour. The rest of the world is asleep. They sit at the dining-room table.

'Hungry?' asks her mother.

'No,' says Joss.

'Tired?'

'Not really.'

Her mother doesn't know what to say. Joss understands because she doesn't either. It's different.

Her mother opens her purse and takes out a little plastic bottle with two pills in it.

'Here, take one of these. It'll help you sleep.' Joss puts the tiny pill on her tongue. It's bitter. She swallows it down with her tea.

Her mother takes her upstairs and tucks her in. Joss doesn't want to go to sleep. Her mother sits on the end of the bed and leans back against the wall. She rubs Joss's feet. Joss's eyes keep shutting. The sleeping tablet drags her under.

Panic in the place of dreams. Wake. Wake. Climb the ladder, wake. The hole in the ground will not open. The grass will not lift. The ladder snaps. Pieces tumble in darkness. She cannot wake.

Morning

Joss wakes. The sunlight is too bright. Her mother is sitting on the end of her bed. Brakes screech. A car honks. It's late. Joss sits up. Her mother has tears in her eyes, she holds out her arms, Joss crawls down the bed to her.

'He's dead,' her mother says and begins to cry, really cry. She wraps Joss in her arms and rocks her back and forth. Joss feels her mother's heart against her own and a scream breaks from her belly that has no sound. Her body convulses like the earth in quake and tears burst from her eyes, silently.

People arrive as though a smoke signal had been sent up. How did they know? Her mother must have phoned. Joss doesn't remember her mother using the phone.

Uncle Rupert takes over. Aunty Irene makes tea. Uncle Bob sits her mother down. They have presents for Joss. Big ones; dolls and girl things.

'For your birthday,' says Uncle Rupert stroking Joss's hair. Joss is confused. Don't they understand her father is dead. Joss looks to her mother. Uncle Ted is between them. There's a knock on the door, Aunty Irene answers. It's Barry.

'Oh Jesus, Irene,' he says and hugs her. He sees Joss's mother over Irene's shoulder and heads straight for her.

'Clair', he says and begins to cry. Her mother comforts him. Uncle Rupert pours Barry a scotch.

Joss wonders what they're all doing here. Why don't they go away. He was her father. She goes upstairs. There are too many people.

The gutting knife her father gave her is on the windowsill. Joss picks it up. The blade catches the sunlight. She turns it over in her hand. She can still smell fish on it. She sits on the end of her bed, the presents beside her, and stares out the window. The sky is solid blue and cloudless. Joss gets lost in the blue.

Suddenly her mother is beside her, picking up pieces of the presents Joss has carved. The knife is still in Joss's hand. She hadn't meant to cut up her birthday presents. Uncle Rupert is standing in the doorway. 'Jocelyn, would you like to spend today with a friend? There's a lot your mother's got to do.'

Joss shrugs.

'Good girl.'

Her mother phones Joss's friend's mother.

Timmy and the Princess say they'll drive Joss there. 'Where did they come from?' the thought is vague in Joss's mind. She takes her red jumper. The wind is cold.

They get lost. Joss thought she knew the way. Timmy asks directions at a petrol station. They wind their way out of backstreets crowded by factories and abandoned houses onto the wide roads of South Melbourne. Across the railway line is Joss's friend's house.

Timmy goes to the door. Joss waits in the car. The Princess smiles at her. She doesn't know what to say. Her friend's mother comes to the car. She takes Joss by the hand and leads her through the house.

'Melanie's in the garden,' she says opening the back door. Joss goes outside.

Her friend is sitting on the dunny roof underneath the lemon tree. Joss climbs up. Her friend is ripping up leaves. Joss sits down next to her. They look at each other. Her friend shrugs, 'We're both the same now.'

A Magic Man

'As Hamlet, he was unbelievable.' Barry throws back the last of his drink.

'God, he had an evil sense of humour.' Aurora looks at Joss's mother. 'Remember *Gauguin?*'

Her mother laughs, 'Oh that was awful. I thought Rose would never speak to him again.'

Aurora is staying with them. She is working for her mother.

'What happened?' asks Ellen. Ellen has taken over her mother's job, casting. Her mother has taken over her father's job.

'We used to live in this flat in Sydney, upstairs from Rose and Gary. We'd all been to see *Gauguin;* great play but very disturbing. Well, Richard couldn't resist. He went downstairs to Rose and Gary's, got down on his knees and knocked on the door. Poor Rose knew Richard's knock, and he was six-foot three, so when she opened the door she was looking up and no-one was there.

'Down here ma chérie', he said in his best French accent and nearly gave Rose a heart attack. She burst into tears and didn't speak to him for two weeks.'

Everyone laughs.

'He must have been an amazing man,' says Ellen.

'He was.' Barry raises his glass.

'Would you like to see some photos?' asks Joss's mother.

'Yeah, I'd love to.'

'Honey, grab the two top albums will you.'

Joss goes and gets the photo albums. She puts them on the table in front of her mother. Her mother flips open the album.

'This is when we were in France. And this was a very bad production of *The Crucible*, Richard and I were in.'

Ellen pours over the photographs. Everyone talks over each other, remembering things about her father.

'He was a very handsome man,' says Ellen. 'Joss looks so like him.' Everyone turns and looks at Joss.

'Yes she does,' says her mother.

Joss smiles. She has big feet. She keeps her parents' secrets in her shoes.

BRACELET HONEYMYRTLE
Judith Fox

Shortlisted in the *Australian/*Vogel Literary
Award

'Wonderfully sustained . . . the sense of
fulfilment achieved in simple reflection is
marvellous.'

Jill Kitson

'A splendid, moving book.'

Andrew Riemer

Annie Grace is an old woman. She tends her
garden, and cares for a baby, her great
great-niece, Kimberley. It is a quiet life.

Born into a strict Christian family in Sydney
at the start of the century, Annie contends
with an overbearing mother and a harsh
religion. Yet something stirs under the starch
of faith. Annie finds a friend late in life and
discovers a passion for living to equal her
passion for gardening. In her sixties, Annie
confronts her mother.

This is the story of one woman's struggle to
lay claim to her own life. And within the
seemingly narrow contours of family and
church and garden, Annie discovers that it is,
after all, a big life.

1 86373 850 9

SWIMMING IN SILK
Darren Williams

Winner of the *Australian*/Vogel Literary
Award

'Highly evocative . . . what captivates is the
landscape.'

Jill Kitson

'The writing is an absolute pleasure, creating
an atmosphere that draws the reader in.'

Marele Day

Brilliant skies, sudden storms, black nights
and a ramshackle house that is disintegrating
into the rainforest. Sheltering from their
pasts, Cliff, Susan, Daniel and Jade
experience a few oddly idyllic days and
nights together in the small coastal town two
of them call home and to which the others
have returned.

Swimming in Silk is an extraordinarily
evocative and sensual novel about the
mysterious and intricate relationship between
people, the elements, and the land in which
they live.

1 86373 849 5

THE SUNKEN ROAD
Garry Disher

The Sunken Road is a moving, powerful novel set in the wheat and wool country of mid-north South Australia. At once the story of a region, a town and a people, it is also the story of Anna Tolley who lives through momentous changes and earns the envy, love and hatred of those around her.

1 86448 074 2